James Murdoch, François-Thomas-Marie d'Arnaud

## The Tears of Sensibility

Vol. I

James Murdoch, François-Thomas-Marie d'Arnaud

**The Tears of Sensibility**
*Vol. I*

ISBN/EAN: 9783337030797

Printed in Europe, USA, Canada, Australia, Japan

Cover: Foto ©Andreas Hilbeck / pixelio.de

More available books at **www.hansebooks.com**

# THE

# TEARS of SENSIBILITY,

## NOVELS:

NAMELY,

1. THE CRUEL FATHER.
2. ROSETTA; OR, THE FAIR PENITENT REWARDED.
3. THE RIVAL FRIENDS.
4. SIDNEY AND SILLI; OR, THE MAN OF BENEVOLENCE AND THE MAN OF GRATITUDE.

Tranflated from the French of

## M. D' ARNAUD,

## BY JOHN MURDOCH.

## VOL. I.

## LONDON:

Printed for EDWARD and CHARLES DILLY, in the Poultry.

MDCCLXXIII.

# ADVERTISEMENT.

IF there are novels which deserve to be admitted into the closet of a reader of taste, they are those surely in which sentiment is blended with incident; and, to the honour of these days be it remarked, such only attain that distinction.

Of this kind are the following pieces of M. D' Arnaud; who, though he has been for years the favourite novelist of the continent, has yet remained almost a stranger in England. If the admirers of Nature in her simplicity should object, that, in some passages, he has, from a warmth of fancy, over-leaped the strict boundaries of probability; that, in others,

others, where the characters are Englifh, we ftill difcover the manners and the cuftoms of France ; yet infenfible muft be that mind, which does not feel, through every page, the philofopher, and the man of genius.

To thofe who may be inclined to compare, with rigid accuracy, the form in which thefe novels are now prefented to the world, with that in which they appeared originally, or who may entertain inadequate ideas of tranflation; it may not be improper to obferve, that the phrafe and diction of M. D' Arnaud, though they are defervedly held in eftimation, are yet fo *fentimentally* refined, fo truely *Parifian*, in many places, as to obftruct every effort to naturalize them

in

in a foreign tongue. Regardlefs of the letter, therefore, the only ftudy of the Tranflator has been, to catch the fpirit, of his original; to adopt fuch expreffions, and to employ fuch a mode of compofition, as he conceived that the ingenious author would have adopted, would have employed, if he had written for an Englifh reader. He has even varied, where it might be done with advantage, a few of the many fituations which appeared to him, from a load of colouring, to border upon the unnatural.—With what propriety he has prefumed to take thefe freedoms, prefumed to attempt the tranflation of an author, who has been repeatedly pronounced incapable of tranflation, the candid and intelligent will with juftice determine.

# E R R A T A.

## V O L.  I.

*Page* 13. *line* 7. force, *read*, ardour.

P. 111. *l.* 13. appendages which, *r.* appendages to it which.

P. 149. *l.* 2. cauſe their, *r.* cauſe of their.

P. 150. *laſt line*, enamoured with, *r.* enamoured of.

## V O L.  II.

*Page* 3. *line* 9. vice, *read*, view.

P. 8. *l.* 3. enamoured with, *r.* enamoured of.

P. 31. *l.* 9. penetrate the, *r.* penetrate into the.

P. 73, *l.* 4 *from the bottom*, relinquiſhes, *r.* relinquiſh.

P. 134. *l.* 11. by an exterior ſhow, *r.* by a ſhow.

P. 149. *l.* 2 *from the bottom*, dele *ever*.

# CRUEL FATHER.

VIRTUE and Difcretion, while they require that young perfons fhould maintain a ftrict guard againft the dangerous influence of the paffions, impofe obligations equally ftrong upon parents. The foibles of youth, a feafon incapable of reflection, and denied the grand leffon of experience, ought to be corrected with a gentle hand. The authority of a father, they tell us, is an image of that of the divine being upon earth. Surely then man cannot, in his imperfect ftate, make a more near approach to

the dignity of that being, than by reftrain-
ing every idea that borders upon rigour,
than by giving an unbounded fcope to the
dictates of lenity and benevolence. Befides,
the foothing remonftrances of a father or a
mother leave a more deep impreffion on the
hearts of children, than threats and feverity;—feverity, which, by rendering them defperate, frequently hurries them from one
fault, which might have been foon repaired,
into another, till they are at length loft in
a labyrinth of infamy and guilt.

Of thefe truths the ftory of Lady Harriet
Somerfet exhibits a ftriking inftance; and
it ought to be an eternal monitor to parents.
To the advantages of birth, and the profpect
of an ample fortune, Lady Harriet joined
the moft engaging accomplifhments. Her
every look and gefture breathed a charm,
which even beauty cannot impart, a fenfibility, which is more frequently the fource
of pain than of pleafure, and which, though

de-

delightful to the objects of it, is yet generally fatal to thofe who poffefs it.  Her heart
was formed for love ; and fhe had fo happily
blended the graces of the mind with thofe of
fentiment and figure, that fhe was confidered as the model of perfection.  She was as
yet in her cradle when fhe loft a mother, by
whom fhe was idolized.  Fathers are ftrangers to the refinements of maternal love ;
and to the death of the Countefs of Somerfet, the misfortunes of Lady Harriet may,
in a great meafure, be attributed.  The
earl educated his daughter himfelf ; and
though fhe was dear to him as his life, he
yet never fpoke to her but in the rigid tone
of a mafter : a conduct, which intimidates
young minds, and which depraves more often
than it reforms.  Lady Harriet never faw
her father but fhe trembled.  To the ftern-
nefs of his difpofition his lordfhip added an
unfufferable pride.  Sprung, as he fuppofed
himfelf, from the ancient chieftains of Bri-
tain, he determined that one of the firft peers

of

of the realm alone fhould prefume to addrefs
his daughter ; and he never once conceived
that Lady Harriet would feel the impreffion
of love till fhe had received the fanction of
his authority.—Amazing prepoffeffion in parents, as if the heart could expand or con-
tract itfelf at their pleafure !

Mr. Belford, a merchant of credit, and a
member for one of the Cornifh boroughs,
frequently waited upon the earl. His fon
occafionally accompanied him ; and it was
not long before Lady Harriet felt a difappointment each time the youth did not appear. She became thoughtful ; and when
fhe fpoke, it was to enquire about young
Belford, whofe image forfook her not even
in fleep. As yet, however, fhe was a ftranger to the nature of her fentiments. She
only knew that fhe was happy in the prefence of Belford, miferable in his abfence. Nature had lavifhed upon this
young gentleman thofe gifts which captivate

vate the heart, a fine shape, noble and engaging features, eyes, which at once expreffed vivacity and languor; that affecting
timidity of fentiment, which is fuperior to
all the parade of wit, that kind of magic,
in fine, which affects, which attracts, and
which cannot be expreffed, animated his
whole frame. Fortune, lefs propitious,
had denied him the imaginary luftre of
birth, and that of opulence, which is
equally unfubftantial, when people have
learned to fet a proper value upon the illu-
fions of humanity. In the eyes of the
Earl of Somerfet, thefe were effential
difadvantages. His daughter, however, faw
through a different medium. She confulted
her heart alone; and Love, who pays but
little attention to birth or fortune, told her,
that Mr. Belford was the moft amiable of
men. The Earl had no idea that his daughter had fo much as obferved the youth; and
he thought it impoffible that a young lady
of quality could be fufceptible of the leaft

emotion in favour of the fon of a commoner :—as if Nature had eftablifhed thcfe chimerical diftinctions, and as if all men poffeffed not an equal right to experience fenfibility, and to excite it !

Lady Harriet, without yet enquiring, or even wifhing to enquire, into the fituation of her heart, became more and more a flave to her paffion for Belford. She felt a continued increafe of pleafure each time fhe faw him, of mifery at his departure. With what propriety is Love reprefented with a bandage over his eyes ! He puts it on with his own hands. He refembles a fire which appears not till it has become a conflagration, when it is hardly poffible to extinguifh it.

Unhappily the fouls of this young couple were congenial. Though awed by the dignity of her fituation, yet Belford loved Lady Harriet with a tendernefs unbounded as her

own.

own. Hardly could he conceal his emotion when he faw her; and when their eyes accidentally met, his whole frame feemed to be convulfed. She happened one day to touch his hand; and he inftantly fell in a fwoon at her feet, in the prefence of a numerous company, who, though alarmed at the accident, were yet ftrangers to the caufe of it. The more he endeavoured to forget his dear Lady Harriet, the more fhe clung to his heart; nor was it long before the agitation of his fpirits threw him into a diforder, which feemed to promife a fpeedy period to his mifery. His father, who had no other child, fupported him in his arms, whilft he watered him with his tears.

" Charles," faid he to him tenderly, " open to me thy heart. Thy illnefs proceeds from a melancholy which has preyed upon thee for above thefe fix months, though I, thy father, am a ftranger to its fource. Often have I obferved a tear in thy eye

ready

ready to ſtart—henceforth pour all thy ſorrows into my boſom.  Say but the word,
my dear child, and my fortune, inconſider-
able as it is, my trade, ſhall inſtantly be
thine.——I cannot be unhappy while I am
thy benefactor and friend."

" Alas !  Sir," replied the youth, " people
die. not from a deſire of wealth :—all I have
to beg is, a continuance of that love, which
—I wiſh I could merit—but my heart——

His  tears fell ſo, faſt that he could ſpeak
no more.  In vain did his father urge him
to explain himſelf.  He accidentally mentioned the Earl of Somerſet.  At the ſound
of that name,  the afflicted youth ſprung up,
as if from the arms of death ;  and, after having thrown a languiſhing look upon the author of his exiſtence, and heaved a profound
ſigh, he ſunk back upon his pillow.

The

The secret of his love, however, he still kept inviolate; though, animated perhaps by the profpect of being one day beloved, he, in a little time, began to recover. Love feldom exifts without hope—hope, which of all our errors is the moft delufive.

It would be no eafy tafk to defcribe the condition of Lady Harriet during the above interval. Then, and not till then, did she difcover that her feelings for Belford were thofe of a love the moft tender and paffionate. There were moments in which she wifhed to triumph over her weaknefs, to liften to reafon and duty; to comply, in fhort, with a prejudice, to which Cuftom has rendered it neceffary to fubmit. But her whole force and fupport she borrowed from herfelf; and every thing, of courfe, betrayed her. Sometimes she deceived herfelf fo far, as to believe that her anxiety about Belford was merely the effect of pity.—With what joy did she learn that he was reftored to life,

that

that she should see him again ! Transports like these could not fail to open her eyes to a passion, which, violent as it was, she yet endeavoured to disguise under the garb of compassion.

Belford had hardly recovered, when he directed his steps to a park in the neighbourhood of Somerset Castle, where Lady Harriet often walked. No sooner had he reached her favourite spot, than Fancy presented to him the print of her steps. In one place, he recollected that she had gathered flowers; in another, that she had stopped to admire a prospect; and a little further, there was a canal, on the border of which she had once reclined, and in which he still beheld her image. So powerful is the enchantment of love in its infancy, that these minute circumstances, so insipid, so unmeaning, to the generality of mankind, are the source of so many raptures which intoxicate every heart that truly feels its soft impressions.

Bel-

Belford had chofen the moft retired path.
It is in love alone that we can tafte the
fweets of folitude, that we can prefer the
foothing languor which attends it, to the
turbulent enjoyments of fociety.—Delightful
enthufiafm! how exquifite muft be the
pleafure which can make us fenfible of thy
charms! Belford gave himfelf wholely up to
it. His foul, impatient of reftraint, panted
for its enlargement.

"Alas!" faid he, throwing himfelf upon
the grafs, while tears almoft ftopped his utterance; " alas! of what folly and madnefs
am I guilty, in cherifhing a paffion which
I ought to fupprefs!——a paffion which
can never be gratified but with guilt! Every
idea of hope is vain. Lady Harriet, Lady
Harriet! thy empire over my heart is unbounded. Life were, to me, beneath a
thought, could I be permitted to declare
with what ardour, what refpect, I love thee.
——Shall none but thofe of noble birth
adore the daughter of Lord Somerfet?——
Would

Would I were a monarch, that I might have the pleafure of placing her upon a throne, of refigning it to her, of confirming her the abfolute miftrefs of my foul!——Whither does Fancy carry me!——I have no pretenfions but what I owe to the induftry of my father.——I am nothing—Lady Harriet is every thing.——Yet fhall my refpect for her remain inviolate.——Yes, I would fooner die than declare to her my love—would die contented, if my eyes, ere they are clofed for ever, could obtain one glance, one momentary glance, of her's."

" Mr. Belford!" cried Lady Harriet; who, conducted by chance to the fame fpot, had heard the tender exclamations of her lover ; " Mr. Belford!" cried fhe, and fhe could not utter another word. She retreated a few fteps, in order to withdraw, when, oppreffed by a variety of emotions, fhe dropped down. Belford threw himfelf at her feet.

" My

" My secret, then, adorable Lady Harriet, is at length revealed to you!—Yes, madam, I do love, adore, you. Though I feel that I am the most audacious, the most culpable, of men, that I am an object unworthy of your notice, yet I feel with infinitely more ——, that the passion you have kindled in my bosom can never be extinguished. Deign, at least, to raise upon me those eyes—those eyes, from which I have imbibed that love which is my only crime. Will you be so ungenerous as not to pardon me?—Pardon me!—No: quick, inform my lord of my unparalleled presumption. I deserve the severest punishment.—But Death will come to my relief, and you perhaps—perhaps will pity me—"

" Pity you!" interrupted Lady Harriet, with all the extatic languor of love, and with her bewitching eyes riveted upon her lover; " pity you! Ah! Belford, Belford! we were both born to be wretched !"

Lady

Lady Harriet, no longer miftrefs of herfelf, avowed her paffion. The pride of
rank, reafon, decency, virtue, fhe at once
facrificed to love. They interchanged a
thoufand vows of eternal conftancy, while
they yielded to an enthufiafm which no language can exprefs, and which innocence
alone can feel.

On her return homeward, Lady Harriet
began to open her eyes on the imprudence
of her conduct, and to view its confequences
in their utmoft extent.

" Wretch that I am," exclaimed fhe,
" to what lengths has the fhameful influence
of an unworthy paffion hurried me—a paffion, which, inftead of concealing in my
own breaft, I have declared to the object of
it, though it is impoffible that he fhould
ever be my hufband ?——What will my father, my friends, the world, fay ?——What
fhall I fay to myfelf, if I liften one moment

to the dictates of Reason or of Honour?——
Reason, Honour! Alas! thefe cannot render me infenfible to the united charms of
Virtue and the Graces. To fee Belford, and
not to love him, is an impoffibility.—How
refpectful, how refined, are his fentiments!—
Engroffed by paffion, whofe fweets fhall
be unembittered by remorfe, mutual love
will conftitute our happinefs. We will exift folely for each other. My father will
not compel me to marry; and I fhall retain
my duty to him inviolate, by permitting no
freedoms that are either unworthy of my
rank, or inconfiftent with my honour.——
Is there any real enjoyment that is not founded in fentiment?——No. I fhall fee Mr.
Belford——fhall fee him, and hear that he
loves me.——In the core of my heart will
I cherifh him.——I fhall be the happieft of
women."

Thus it is that we fuffer the firft tranfports of Love to fteal upon our hearts. We
imagine

imagine that we can fix boundaries to our paſſions; and while Reaſon ſeems to come to our aſſiſtance, we advance to a precipice from which we find ourſelves no longer able to retreat.

Our lovers often met in the park, in the very ſpot where they had told each other they loved ; a circumſtance which, in their eyes, gave it an inexpreſſible charm. At firſt, they knew no enjoyments but thoſe of innocence and ſenſibility. The happineſs of Belford was at its height, when he held in his hands, or covered with his kiſſes, the flowers which his Harriet had gathered, or which had adorned her boſom. With what rapture did he ſmell the fragrance of them, did he preſs them to his heart !—Delighful ſenſations !——ſenſations, which hearts that have been blunted by diſſipation can never feel, never know that they exiſt but by the convulſive impulſes of art.

It

It is not in man to be satisfied with the
pure affection which subsists among aëri-
al beings. Our young couple experienced
this truth. Their desires, as they became
less delicate, became more bold and impe-
tuous.—Innocence, one of the fairest gifts
of heaven, forsook them ; Nature was as yet
too strong for Reason; situation and circumstances were favourable; and at length Lady
Harriet, forgetting the duty she owed to her
father and her family, in contempt of the
dictates of Honour and Religion, resigned
herself to the embraces of Mr. Belford.

It was just that punishment should closely
follow guilt.——What an aweful lesson to
young people, who cannot arm themselves
with due vigour against the encroachments
of love ! The feelings of Lady Harriet,
when she found that it was no longer pos-
sible either to repair or to conceal her shame,
are not to be expressed. A stranger to that
repose, which Misery cannot tear from the

bofom of Innocence, fhe perpetually beheld her father ready to facrifice her to his injured honour. The noife which her infamy would make, rung in her ears : fhe felt herfelf the moft wretched and the moft criminal of women. Often did fhe refolve to clofe her forrows in death ; but the powerful fenfations of a mother, which fhe already felt, and the thoughts of parting with Belford, to whom her fituation was ftill unknown, with-held her hand.——With what diftraction did fhe at length inform him of her pregnancy ! with what horror did he receive the fatal intelligence ! He remained frantic with grief ; and no fooner did he feem to have recovered his reafon, than he ran to a fword which prefented itfelf before him. It was already in his hand, when Lady Harriet, flying to him, and holding him by the arm, fhrieked out,

" Heavens ! Mr. Belford, what would you do ?——Is it not enough that I fuffer a thoufand deaths ?"

" And

"And would you have me," replied Belford, with a gloomy wildnefs ;" would you
have me live a moment after having deprived you, not only of your honour, but your
reputation? Ah! Lady Harriet, I am thy
murderer !———I am"———

A rivulet of tears ftreamed from his eyes;
and he fell, almoft fenfelefs, at her feet.

Dear Belford," refumed Lady Harriet,
" thy diftrefs heightens mine. Think not
I mean to reproach thee. No : 'tis I alone
who am to blame.--To my tendernefs for thee
I have facrificed my rank, my father; have
facrificed honour and heaven. Let thy
love, therefore, fupply the place of thefe ;
let it confole me ; let it make amends to
me, if it is poffible, for all I fuffer. We
talk of dying, Belford!—Alas! is it not
our duty to live, for the fake of the fad fruit
of our affection ?——Ah ! my friend, I already

ready feel myfelf a mother.—Let us not defpair of foftening my lord. I will throw myfelf at his feet; I will embrace his knees; I will water them with my tears. He will pity my fituation; he will permit me to call thee hufband; the innocent babe in my womb will make him hear its voice; it will affect him; and, in confideration of our child, he will pardon me.

Lady Harriet was far from poffeffing that refolution with which fhe would have infpired her hufband. She had not power to make fuch a confeffion to her father. Often had fhe refolved, while the earl queftioned her about the caufe of her melancholy, to throw herfelf before him, with a full difcovery of her fatal fecret; but ftill fhe found herfelf unable to move, ftill the words died upon her lips.

She now blamed her cowardice; and, on her return to her apartment, fhe determined to redouble her efforts. But at the fight of her father, her fears returned; and an accident foon convinced her that they were too well grounded. At the recital of a ftory fimilar to her own, the haughty lord exclaimed, " Had I been that father, my daughter fhould not have furvived a moment."——— From thefe words the wretched Lady Harriet forefaw her fate. Her pregnancy advanced; and, in hopes of an afylum from his fury, fhe refolved to fly from her father to an uncle of her hufband.

Old Belford was now dead; and, from the many loffes he had fuftained in trade, the little all he left behind him was found infufficient for his creditors. The young gentleman, become, as it were, the adopted fon of a relation, foon felt that he no longer had a father, and that Nature alone can either confer that title, or fupport the rights of it. The uncle, a flave to avarice, that ruft which fo often adheres to the fouls of

men of bufinefs, feared the vengeance of
Lord Somerfet, feared that he would in-
volve him in a law fuit; and, abandoning
the young couple to all the bitternefs of
their deftiny, he immediately turned them
out of doors.

The earl was equally grieved and aftonifhed at the elopement of his daughter.
His haughtinefs and feverity could not fupprefs the feelings of a father. All his enquiries and conjectures were fruitlefs. He
was inconfolable, when a vifit from Doctor Willis, a clergyman, diftinguifhed by
his beneficence and genuine piety, was
announced to him. The venerable man
was ufhered in; and, having defired the
Earl to difmifs his attendants, he thus addreffed him:

" My Lord," faid he, " you know that
it is our office to be the interpreters of forrow and adverfity; and I come to pour
their

their tears into your bofom. I might call
the facred power of religion to my aid; but
at prefent I mean only to plead the caufe of
humanity. —— Our heavenly father, my
Lord, is ready and willing to forgive; and
his goodnefs is, perhaps, fuperior even to
his greatnefs. Your daughter——

" My daughter !" interrupted the impatient Earl.

" Wifhes, my Lord, to throw herfelf at
your feet. Overwhelmed with defpair, fhe
would die with pleafure, could fhe obtain
your pardon for her tranfgreffion."

" What tranfgreffion !"

" The greateft that can be committed,"
continued the worthy doctor. " Lady
Harriet pretends not to exculpate herfelf:
fhe confeffes her guilt in its utmoft extent;
and therefore, inftead of your affection, fhe
only

only implores that pity, which we ought
not to refuſe to the meaneſt, the moſt
guilty, of wretches.——Your Lordſhip will
not ſurely caſt her from you !"

The earl melted.

" Then tell me her crime.—I am a father," added his Lordſhip, in a tone full of
of tenderneſs ; " and——and I ſhall forgive
her."

" You will forgive her !" exclaimed the
doctor in a tranſport.

" Doubtleſs I ſhall."

And raiſing his voice, " Madam," continued the venerable paſtor, " you may now
appear."

Lady Harriet immediately entered, followed by her huſband, and threw herſelf at
her father's feet.

" Be-

" Behold your daughter, my Lord," refumed the doctor, " ready to die with grief
and remorfe for her prefumption in marrying
without your confent."

" To whom, to whom, is fhe married ?"
demanded Lord Somerfet, agitated by a variety of emotions.

" That gentleman is her hufband," anfwered he, pointing to Belford.

" Yes, my Lord, my father," cried Lady
Harriet, fhedding a torrent of tears ; " I
have committed a fault, a heinous fault !
Alas ! I am feverely punifhed for it, and
have endeavoured to repair it. Mr. Belford is a man of virtue ; he refpects you ;
we fhall be always obedient to you. We
are your children, deny us not your bleffing."

The

The earl, who till now had been feated, and engroffed by a crowd of jarring paffions, ftarted up with impetuofity.

" That ignoble fellow thy hufband!— Wretch ! get thee from my prefence, and with thee carry my curfe."——

" Ah ! my father, hold thy hand !——

Somerfet had already unfheathed his fword, in order to plunge it into the heart of Belford, who lay proftrate at his feet. Lady Harriet, throwing herfelf, all pale and difhevelled, between her father and her huf- band; " On me," cried fhe, " on me, my " Lord, let thy vengeance fall. I alone am guilty; I alone have deferved death. The only favour I have to beg is, that thou wilt fpare me till I am delivered of an inno- cent babe, who will feel for thee all my ten- dernefs, and be a ftranger to my remorfe."

His

His Lordship had fallen back upon his chair in a fit.   On his recovery,

" Still," faid he, " do I fee thee in this place, this place which thou difhonoureft ? If thou regardeft thy life, fly, fly with thy bafe paramour, and fhare with him the reward of thy crime.———Hence from this caftle, all of you, ye mifcreants, elfe will I drive you from it headlong."

In vain did Doctor Willis attempt to be heard. The diftracted Lady Harriet retreated a few fteps, and returned, exclaiming with a voice choaked with fobs, " Thy curfe, my father!"

" Father! thou haft no father," replied the indignant earl.

And they all three retired, Lady Harriet led by the doctor, in a fwoon, whilft Belford

ford, himfelf ready to fink under the weight of his diftrefs, fupported her in his arms.

Doctor Willis was one of thofe few ec-clefiaftics who, by practifing the duties which they inculcate, are worthy' to approach the altar. It was under his roof that Lady Harriet and Belford had taken fhelter, in hopes of recovering, through his mediation, the favour of my Lord ; and it was by his perfuafion that they had accompanied him to Somerfet Caftle. This worthy man thought he had gained the lucky moment for foftening the earl, when he gave the fignal for their entrance; and Lady Harriet might perhaps have obtained her pardon, paternal love might perhaps have triumphed, if the pride of his lordfhip,wounded at the fight of Belford as his fon-in-law, had not deftroyed this return of tendernefs, and rekindled his utmoft fury.

Lady

Lady Harriet trembled for the life of her hufband. The doctor did not content himfelf with bewailing their diftreffes, and fhedding tears with them. He gave them every affiftance that was in his power; and knowing the danger to which they were expofed, while they continued with him, he provided them with letters to a female relation he had at a village about forty miles from Norwich, where they at length arrived through by-paths, purfued by fear, and almoft motionlefs with fatigue.

They had not been long gone, when Dr. Willis received a meffage to return to Somerfet Caftle. Hardly had he reached the earl's apartment, when his lordfhip exclaimed, " Come forth, thou vile feducer, come forth :—I know how to punifh people of thy complexion ; and thou mayeft expect my utmoft vengeance if thou doft not give me intelligence of this daughter, unworthy of

my

my name, and of the villain who has un-
done her.—Where are they?"

Then did the magnanimity and courage
of Willis break forth in all their fplendour.

" My Lord, I am no feducer; I am the
comforter, the protector, of the unhappy.
Your daughter applied not to me, till after
her marriage to Mr. Belford. I am no
ftranger to the duties which are incumbent
upon children to their parents. Had I feen
Lady Harriet in the infancy of her paffion,
I fhould undoubtedly have exerted every
effort to withdraw her from the abyfs into
which fhe has plunged herfelf; I fhould
have enforced not only the dictates of reafon, but the authority of heaven, which
feems to be invefted with thofe who have
given us birth. But, obliged to commit one
fault to atone for another yet more heinous,
in a word, obliged to marry Mr. Belford,
she

fhe threw herfelf before me for protection.
This, my Lord, I gave her, and in giving
it, I have fulfilled my duty, my inclination.
Compaffion prompted me to it, and God
himfelf commanded it—commanded, that I
fhould not abandon to your fury this unhappy pair.—My lord, I *do* know their retreat—
know it, but never will divulge it."—

" Not divulge it !——Thinkeft thou I
want the means to render thee pliant to my
will ?"—

" Thou fhalt never tear the fecret from
my breaft," continued the other with a noble
firmnefs.

" I fhall punifh thee, however.——Here,
my fervants !"———

" Call them," interrupted the doctor
with the utmoft compofure ; ——·—" call
them.——Relent not at fight of my grey
hairs. Death fhall not force me to betray a

hap-

haplefs couple, fo deferving of your favour.
—Beware left a day fhould come, when
Nature fhall find a paffage to your heart,
and find you unable to obey her commands.
Believe me, the neglected duties of a parent
will not pafs unpunifhed. Sooner or later
you will feel compunction :———heaven
grant that it may not be fruitlefs !"———

The earl, no longer able to contain himfelf, thruft the venerable old man from his
prefence. But Dr. Willis was not to be
difmayed by fuch mortifications ; and his
fteady conduct may convince us, that true
piety is fuperior to human courage, that its
principles are immoveable.

How different were the religious principles
of Mrs. Crofts, his relation at Norwich, to
whom he had recommended our young
couple'! ——— Mrs. Crofts confidered herfelf
as a model of chriftian perfection. Guilt-
lefs of indifcretion, as her heart was form-

ed

ed rather for hatred than for love, she felt a pleasure in disclaiming every species of sensibility. Her husband, who had fallen a victim to the virulence of her temper, and to her pride, left her a widow, with a child whom she cruelly oppressed. Scrupulously attached to the forms of religion, she neglected the spirit and the maxims of it; and she found a greater pleasure in being seated in the most conspicuous part of the church, than in giving her mite toward the relief of the unfortunate.——The doctor knew not her character but by Fame;—Fame, which, so liable are we to be imposed upon by shew and grimace, was lavish in her praise. There are few who can admire the simplicity of Virtue, though daily observation may convince us that Ostentation is nothing more than the cloke of Vice and of Imposture.

The doctor had mentioned to his kinswoman the motives of Lady Harriet and her hus-

band for quitting the place of their nativity.
Even in receiving her new guefts, this fu-
rious bigot could not fupprefs her zeal.
She perpetually declaimed againft the
wickednefs of clandeftine marriages, perpetually fought for, and was happy when
fhe could obtain, opportunities to diftrefs
this unfortunate couple. But fhe fuffered
not the whole venom of her cruel devotion
to burft forth, till fhe perceived that they
began to be in want of money. She then
found it impoffible to live any longer with
people, " whom the Lord feemed to have
caft off;" and in a little time fhe reduced
them to the neceffity of flying from her
houfe.

Lady Harriet, who was now at the point
of her delivery, forefaw an unavoidable fe-
ries of diftrefs open itfelf before her. Their
mifery feemed to be at an height.——What
were the fenfations of Belford !—Had himfelf been the only victim of this torrent of

mif-misfortunes, he could have supported it with some degree of firmness: but he beheld, sinking before his eyes, a woman whom he adored;—a woman who ought not to have known sorrow or indigence even by name, and who had been reduced to these dreadful extremities by her love for him;—extremities, which, thanks to our want of philosophy and humanity, are almost always attended with a reproach, a contempt, that are infinitely more intolerable than adversity itself. It is not in man to withstand such trials. Belford could not look at his wife without feeling a thousand daggers at his heart. He had exerted every effort, that is consistent with honour, to extricate him from this gulph of misery; and Fortune had baffled his every hope. At length he returned to his wretched abode, less dejected than usual.

" My dear Harriet," said he, as he embraced her, and clasped her in his arms,

" Heaven

" Heaven has ceafed to frown upon us. Thy days, however, fhall not be cut fhort by hunger. I fhall be enabled to preferve thy life. As for my own, I fhould be regard-lefs of it, if that of all I hold dear did not depend upon it.——Ah ! adorable woman, into what guilt am I plunged by love !"—

Lady Harriet begged to know by what accident their indigence had been relieved ; but the anfwers fhe received were vague and myfterious. He always left her by break of day, and never returned till late at night. She was forced to fwallow her homely meals alone. One morning, having had the cu-riofity to follow him, fhe faw him go into a field, and labour the ground, yoked to a plough. She ftopped fhort, motionlefs with aftonifhment and grief, and knew not if fhe could believe her eyes.

" You need not," cried Belford to his mafter, who ftood befide him, " call in

other

other affiftance ;—I feel myfelf equal to the work of many labourers. Doubt not what I fay.—I have a wife, Sir," continued he to the farmer, with a tear in his eye, " whom I adore—adore, and have yet reduced to the extremity of wretchednefs. All I afk of you is, what may be neceffary for her fubfiftence. Bread and water will fuffice for me ; and I fhall blefs heaven, fo long as my wife does not fuffer."—

" Ah ! my friend," exclaimed Lady Harriet, darting into the arms of her hufband, " Ah ! my friend, what do I fee ?—Is it at this price that I exift !"—

And fhe fobbed forth the reft of her forrows in his bofom. Belford tenderly complained of her curiofity ; and when he had recovered from his agitation,

" Look here, Sir," cried he to the farmer, " and wonder not that I fhould be fo

foli-

folicitous to render my labour acceptable to you.—Alas ! I am the fource of all the misfortunes of this deferving woman :—fhe was not born to know diftrefs like this."—

" I was born, my dear hufband," interrupted Lady Harriet, " to love thee.—Thou art every thing to me.—Let us not talk of grandeur————let us forget dreams which never can be realifed.  I wifh not to entertain a thought of aught but thee, and the unhappy babe to whom I fhall foon give birth.  May Fortune be lefs unfavourable to the fruit of our love than it has been to ourfelves !————But, Belford, I will fooner fuffer an hundred deaths than enjoy an exiftence which cofts thee fo dear."

" Divine creature ! knoweft thou not that Love can accomplifh wonders ?—Continue to preferve for me that heart which is a treafure ; and there is no labour, no fatigue, which I fhall not be able to fupport.

—I

—I will water the earth with my tears, and I shall be happy while I enjoy the affection of my dear Harriet."

Norris, so the farmer was called, was struck with this moving scene. " My children," said he to them, " your situation affects me strongly.—How great are the distresses attendant upon poverty!——how happy should I be to relieve them!——All that I can do is, to prevent you, Belford, from working too hard.——I shall be tender of you as of my own son."——

The primeval innocence of nature seemed to have revived in this venerable old man, whose virtues out-numbered his years. A mild vivacity sparkled in his eyes ; upon his bald forehead were blended that benevolence and dignity which seem to be inseparable from a life that has been spent in the practice of morality. He invited the young couple to dinner ; and they recounted to him ingenuously nuoufly their faults and their misfortunes. Norris returned their franknefs. He preffed them both to his heart, with a warmth which thofe only can conceive, who have been ftrangers to the buftle of cities, or who have been untainted by the fociety of the abandoned.

Lord Somerfet, in the mean time, endeavoured to forget the lofs of his daughter. Deprived of the fweets of paternal love, he devoted his whole foul to the allurements of ambition ; and it was not long before he rofe to the firft pofts in the adminiftration. He lived with a fifter, who cherifhed in him this paffion for pomp and preferment, and who exerted every artifice to root from his memory the unfortunate Lady Harriet. Merely from the profpect of fucceeding to the family eftate, fhe armed her utmoft malice againft the efforts of a tendernefs, which can never be totally fuppreffed, and which perpetually returned

upon

upon the earl, to convince him how infinitely inferior the enjoyments of ambition are to the delightful emotions of nature.

Thefe ought now to have foftencd the cruel fate of Belford. Lady Harriet had born to him a fon; a circumftance which rendered their love yet more ftrong. They nurfed him in their bofom; and by his careffes it feemed as if the little innocent wanted to confole his parents, and to fmile away every frown of Fortune.

"Ah! my child," faid Belford to him as he held him in his arms, and wept over him; "ah! my child, what mifery have I entailed upon thee by giving thee birth!—Thou oweft nothing to me.—And doft thou throw thy little arms around me, my fweet angel!—Alas! I am not worthy to be thy father—I am"——

And he could not proceed for tears.

"My

" My dear Belford," interrupted Lady Harriet," ceafe to torment thyfelf.——Our child will not blame us for the mifery to which we are reduced.—No : he will learn patience from us, and he will mingle his tears with ours.———Alas ! my friend, but for him fhould we have known this dif-trefs ?"—

The worthy farmer took every opportunity to render their fituation lefs difagreeable. Often did Lady Harriet attempt to eafe her hufband of part of his toil. Belford, however, ftill obliged her to defift.

" No, my Harriet," faid he, " let me tear the bofom of the earth, and water it with my tears :—it becomes me. But the daughter of Lord Somerfet fhall never be humbled fo low."

" I

"  I fhould be humbled indeed, Belford," replied fhe, " were I to ceafe to
love thee.———Does not one foul ani-
mate us both ?——It does.——Why then
am I not fuffered to partake of thy toils ?—
Why am I denied the pleafure of being always near to thee, of having thee always before my eyes, of feeling an increafe of love
for thee every day ?"———

Belford was immoveable.——She continued, however, to attend him with his meals,
which fhe dreffed with her own hands, and
which they ate together, with their fon
feated between them, whom they gazed
upon with rapture, and almoft fmothered
with kiffes.

"  Belford," fhe faid to him, " thy
Harriet would never, perhaps, have experienced thefe delicious fenfations, had
fhe been wedded to a proud lord.——Let us
not regret that we are poor ; that we enjoy

not

not the fplendour of rank.—I only regret that.
my father—ah ! why did he with-hold from us
his blefling ?—But I tire you with repetiti-
ons of this. Belford, I am now the happieft of women ; now that I fit by thy fide,
and, without referve, tell thee all my love.
Thefe were the hands which prepared this
fimple repaft for thee.—Our board is not furrounded with falfe or with wicked friends.—
We live in the hearts of each other. Our
dear boy will add to our felicity ; and my
love for thee will fpring up in his heart."

Already did this incomparable woman
feem to have infpired her fon with that in-
genuous delicacy of fentiment which few
can feel, and fewer yet exprefs. Scarce had
he begun to walk, when he ufed to run to
meet his father, to fmile upon him, to ftretch
out to him his little hands, to endeavour, as
it were, to wipe the fweat from his brow, to
cover him with thofe kiffes, fo affecting, fo
delicious, to the paternal heart.

Our

Our young couple feemed to have found a father in the worthy farmer. They enjoyed that virtuous tranquillity, that peace of mind, which conftitute the happinefs of honeft poverty. Their cottage they preferred to the moft fumptuous palace, for it was the manfion of innocence and of genuine love. Forgotten by the world, their thoughts were centered in each other, and in their worthy benefactor; and, regardlefs of their former condition, they had not a wifh beyond what their prefent fituation afforded. This felicity, fo fimple, fo little known, fo little envied, was now, however, near a clofe. The plank which had enabled them to brave the ftorm, was ready to fink under their feet.

Old Norris, already feeble by age, fell into a kind of infenfibility, little different from death; and, Richard, his fon, affumed the management of the farm. Then did the happy days of Belford and his Har-

riet

riet vanifh;——then did they feel themfelves in the actual fituation of day-labour-
ers, abandoned to all the barbarity of an
infolent mafter, who confiders thofe whom
Fortune has placed under him merely as
beafts of burthen. Belford found himfelf
unable for the fatigue; and Lady Harriet,
though nurfed in the bofom of delicacy,
would yet perfift in fharing the labours of
her husband; who, to enliven his ftrength,
often placed his fon at the extremity of a
ridge, by the fide of his mother, on whom
he gazed inceffantly, as at once the objects
and the reward of his toil, and to whom
he often hurried from his labour to weep
over, and to embrace them.——To behold
fuch a fcene and not to feel it, Richard muft
have had a heart of ftone.

" Let me conjure you," faid Lady Harriet to him, one day, throwing herfelf at
his feet, in an agony of grief, " let me conjure you, Sir, in the name of humanity, of

heaven,

heaven, to mitigate the labour of my hufband.——Alas ! all the affiftance which I
can give him is of little avail.——I was not
brought up," added fhe with a torrent of
tears, " to difcharge fuch laborious employments.——"

" Laborious employments !" echoed
Richard in the ftern tone of a barbarian.—
" Believe me, I fhall not give my money
for nothing.——Every fervant of mine fhall
perform his tafk.—Your hufband is young,
and ought to enure himfelf to labour.——
With the money he cofts me, I could maintain a pair of oxen, which would do more
fervice to me."————

" But, Sir, if I fhould lofe him !—

" Well, if you fhould, I fhall find another fervant."————

" Ah !

Ah ! Norris, my worthy Norris," ex-claimed Lady Harriet, as fhe retired, " is this thy fon ?"————

She flew to the venerable old man, who lay upon the bed of death, in hourly expec-tation of relief—flew to him, and told him her diftrefs. The fituation of our unhappy couple feemed to reftore him to life.

" Richard," faid he, " haft thou already forgotten the precepts, the example, I gave to thee ?————Can'ft thou thus cruelly op-prefs an unfortunate pair, who have, in confidence, told me their birth and rank, who deferve thy utmoft compaffion and re-fpect, who ought to have been thy maf-ters."—

" Why, father, I have promifed to em-ploy them fo long as I find them ufeful to me."——

" Ufe-

" Ufeful to thee !—Ah ! Richard, if that is the extent of thy benevolence, dread thy latter end.————Thou wilt die in poverty. ————I fhall die in wealth, a ftranger to re-morfe, and full of confidence in the good-nefs of God.————May he of his mercy foften thee, and pardon thee for thefe inju-ries to humanity !————He who injures that, injures heaven, which, fooner or later, will be revenged.————The moft heinous crime in the eye of the Almighty, is that barbarity for which thou feemeft to applaud, thyfelf. —Ah ! my fon, thy cruelty ftabs me to the heart."————

The good old man had not uttered thefe words many minutes, when he expired—expired, with all the refignation of an ho-neft man, and a real chriftian. His unfeel-ing fon quickly difcharged the funeral offices. Not a day, however, elapfed that Belford and his wife did not dwell upon the virtues of their worthy benefactor, and fhed

tears to his memory. His death yet heightened their diſtreſs, yet heightened the barbarity of their new maſter.

In vain did Belford, already worn out
with fatigue, ſay to himſelf, " It is for my
wife, my ſon, that I labour."—Love, which
till now had worked miracles, could no
longer triumph over Nature. Lady Harriet one day ſurpriſed her huſband in a ditch,
almoſt ſmothered, with his head upon his
knee, and in a ſwoon.

" My dear wife," ſaid he to her with a
faltering voice, when he at length recovered, " I can no more.——I have attempted
impoſſibilities, in order to avert the moment
of my deſtruction :—I now feel the approach
of it.——Thou knoweſt, my Harriet, how
dear thou and our lovely innocent are to
me ; and thou knoweſt that my endeavours
to ſupport the oppreſſions of an inhuman
maſter

master have been unexampled.————I can support them no longer.————I——

At these words, Lady Harriet threw herself, with a scream, into the arms of her husband.

" Ah! my Love," continued Belford, " that body which thou now embracest, will, ere long, be cold.————With what dreadful sensations do I expire!————What will become of thee, of our son?————My God, how great must have been my guilt to have deserved a punishment so rigorous!"————

After an interval of a few minutes, he thus proceeded:

" My worthy friend, endeavour so far to moderate thy grief, as to hear my dying words.————Soon as my eyes are closed, write to my lord; fly to him with thy
child,

child, and, on thy knees, implore his paternal tendernefs.—I feel, my Harriet, what it
is to be a father :—be not difcouraged.——
He will relent, and will pardon thee.——
Tell him that Belford, the caufe of his indignation, is in his grave :—tell him that
he lived, that he died, lamenting the offence
he had given to him ; lamenting, that, by
giving way to love, he had dragged thee into
an abyfs of mifery which thou never fhouldft
have known, and that he would have perifh-
ed with pleafure, if he could have atoned for
his guilt.—Alas ! adorable woman, it is I who
have made thee acquainted with hardfhip,
with reproach, with every indignity which
can attend upon adverfity.—Yet with-hold
not, my Harriet, a tear to my memory,
and reflect that Love was the fource of
all my guilt."——

" And muft I lofe thee !" interrupted his
wife; " is it for me that thou expireft ?—
Ah ! my Belford, it is I who ought to die.—
Should

Should his father be torn from him, what would become of our helplefs babe ?————— Away, my dear husband, with this frightful image of death !——away with it, and put thy truft in heaven, which, ere long, will ceafe to frown upon us !"—

" It is in vain to hope, my Love.————I fubmit to its decrees.—The number of my days is filled up.—From this hour, I fhall never fee thee in this world ; fhall never be able to tell thee, that, if our feelings perifh not with our life, my love for thee fhall be eternal ;——my love, which, hallowed by virtue, by religion, and by adverfity, cannot be offenfive to the fupreme being, and without which my foul fhould be a ftranger to happinefs.—Come to me, my child, and let me embrace thee once more.—Ah ! my little innocent, what an inheritance do I leave to thee !"—

Bel-

Belford pressed his dying lips, sometimes upon the mouth of his son, sometimes upon that of his wife; who, instead of speaking to him, could only clasp him in her arms, with a convulsive tremor, which powerfully expressed the agitation of her mind.

" Tear, my dear wife, tear from me this child. —— The sight of him renders death more terrible to me.——Let me not think of aught but God.—Shall his wrath follow me into the grave ?—The grave !— Here, here in this ditch, let me be interred. —— Adieu ! my Love.——Live to lament me !——May the tenderness of our dear boy remind thee of his father's love ! —Harriet, give me thy hand.——I feel the arm of Death—I——

The distracted wife knew not what to do. —She started back a few steps, as if for affistance ; and ere she could return, Belford had breathed his last sigh.

On

On the recovery of her fenfes, the firft object which ftruck Lady Harriet was one of her fellow-fervants, who, touched with compaffion, endeavoured to confole her.

" Where," cried fhe, " is my husband ?—where is my Belford ?"—

" Alas ! Madam, your husband is no more ; and my mafter has given me orders to difcharge you from his fervice."—

Thefe words were fo many thunderbolts to Harriet. She inftantly fell into another fwoon, from which fhe had hardly recovered, when the inhuman Richard, regardlefs of her fituation, of her tears and fobs, formally pronounced her difmiffion.——— She wandered in fearch of an afylum;—wandered till fhe reached the abode of an indigent cottager, who lived at the diftance of a few miles from the farm : and from thence fhe difpatched a letter to her father, which

con-

contained a minute and a faithful detail of her misfortunes.

Lord Somerfet had, for fome time, become a prey to that uneafinefs, that difcontent, which are the infallible attendants upon ambition. Honours were fo far from fupplying the place of paternal love, that he found his daughter cling to his heart more and more clofely every day. Often, when in company, did he fuddenly retire, in order to give a vent to his tears, to pronounce aloud the name of his Harriet. His inhumanity ftruck him with remorfe; and he no longer beheld but with abhorrence a fifter, who, at every mention of the unfortunate Lady Harriet, bridled with indignation.——Unhappily the above letter fell into the hands of this inhuman relation; and fhe had the addrefs to prevent it from ever reaching thofe of her brother. Daily more and more difgufted at her infolence, which her antipathy to his daughter render-

ed

ed yet more intolerable, his lordſhip began in his turn, to diſcover marks of coldneſs and reſentment; and they, at length, parted, full of indignation at each other.

The earl, ſtill unacquainted with the fate of his daughter, and unable any longer to ſupport his affliction, endeavoured to draw comfort from the converſation of Doctor Willis, the venerable clergyman whom he formerly ſpurned from his preſence, and whom no threats could induce to withdraw, for one moment, his protection from the unhappy.—Though aſtoniſhed when he received an invitation to wait upon his lordſhip, yet the doctor inſtantly ſet out for Somerſet Caſtle. Soon as the earl obſerved him, " Come forward," ſaid he, " thou venerable man :——it is I who ought to be embarraſſed at this interview.—Emboldened by the hope of atoning for the injuſtice of which I have been guilty, and convinced of thy generoſity, I have taken the

liberty

liberty to fend for thee.———Thy prediction is accomplifhed.——I now feel myfelf a father, the moft diftreffed, the moft difconfolate, of fathers.—Canft thou give me any tidings of my daughter?—— Ah! would fhe but return!———I forgive her from my heart —— I will embrace her hufband as my fon."—

The doctor wept.

" With what joy, my Lord, do I perceive that the emotions of a parent, that the rights of Nature and Religion, have refumed poffeffion of your heart!———I will no longer conceal it from you, that I recommended your unfortunate daughter and her hufband to my fifter at Norwich, who has fince informed me, that they had quitted her houfe, and that fhe was an utter ftranger to the place of their retreat."—

" Alas! dear Willis, my heart tells me that they are in diftrefs, tells me that Harriet

daily

daily upbraids me for my barbarity, that perhaps, ere now, she has fallen a victim to it.—Give me, I conjure thee, every information about them that thou canst obtain. ———— Henceforth thou shalt find me more grateful than thou hast hitherto found me oppreſſive and unjuſt."—

And he claſped the worthy clergyman in his arms, who was unable to anſwer him but with the tears of ſenſibility and benevolence.

The doctor immediately wrote to Mrs. Crofts; and though every enquiry about the young couple was fruitleſs, he yet became the boſom-friend of Lord Somerſet, who loaded him with favours, and who made him paſs whole days at the castle. Lady Harriet was their conſtant theme. The whole heart and ſoul of this unhappy father were engroſſed by anxiety and ſorrow ;——

by

by anxiety that he might recover his daughter, by forrow that he had loft her.

As the letter, which her cruel aunt had
intercepted, remained ftill unanfwered,
Lady Harriet no longer entertained a doubt
but that her father's heart was fhut againft
her for ever; and fhe abandoned herfelf
to all the horrors of defpair. She had
ftill flattered herfelf, that her father would
at length relent; for her own feelings told
her that it was impoffible a parent could be
callous to the diftreffes of his own offspring.
—" Can a part of our exiftence, which is
fo dear to us," thought fhe often, throwing
her tearful eyes upon her fon, " excite another fentiment but that of love!——Ah!
my father, fhall there be no period to thy
refentment ?"——

Belford perpetually prefented himfelf before her; and to him fhe addreffed her fobs,
as if he had actually exifted, as if fhe had
actually

actually held him in her arms.——To such a pitch did her misery encreafe, that fhe was at length obliged to have recourfe to the com- paffion of the public.————What a fitua- tion !——The daughter of Lord Somerfet, one of the firft peers of the realm, reduced to the neceffity of begging a morfel of bread ! ——The reader may eafily conceive that ma- ternal love alone could have enabled her to fuftain the horrors of fuch complicated dif- trefs. There is no doubt but that Lady Harriet would have rather fuffered a thoufand deaths than have expofed even the picture of her mifery. But if fhe had funk under her misfortunes, if fhe had loft the courage to live, what would have become of the haplefs innocent, who perpetually covered her with his kiffes and with his tears ?—Ye mothers, who fhall perufe this ftory, your hearts alone can truly feel the fufferings of Harriet !———— May ye never experience difafters fo excruciating and fo humilia- ting !————

As

As this victim of adversity crossed, one
day, a large burying ground, fatigue, or
rather, perhaps, an encrease of melancholy,
at sight of the horrid objects before her, induced her to stop. She sat down under the
vault of an ancient monument, which might
have been called the Asylum of Death. Every thing around diffused that gloomy horror, which forces recollection upon us,
and which fills us with the great idea
of our dissolution.. From the bottom of
this subterraneous mansion were discernible
a long range of tombs and sepulchres, which
ended in a deep pit, where were intermix-
ed heaps of bones and remnants of coffins.
——There did Lady Harriet, might the
expression be indulged, behold herself in
the utmost extent of her sorrow. Her son
was seated by her side; and having remained for some time, petrified, as it were, she
started up and flew towards the pit.—A thousand ideas, a thousand sensations, more awful,
a despair more gloomy, than what she had ever

experienced before, engroffed her foul. Which-
ever way fhe turned, the unavoidable deftiny
of man prefented itfelf to her.———Death
feemed to call upon her from all fides, to
tell her, that it was by his aid alone the
oppreffions of humanity could be removed.
She furveyed the immenfe pit, and exclaimed, as it were tranfported, " Is not that the
gulph, in which all mankind are loft ?———
On what fhall I refolve after I have quitted
this place ?———To drag on the weight of
a miferable, an ignominious, exiftence !—
to beg——what a word !——to beg an humiliating fubfiftence, which I cannot even
obtain !—Why, therefore, may I not de-
pofit in this dungeon the burthen of a
wretched life ?——Heaven, at length, touched with my diftreffes, has undoubtedly
brought me hither for that purpofe.——
Its decrees are manifeft.———It is willing
that my mifery fhould have a period ; and
that period it has fixed to the brink of this
pit. ——— Here then will I die !——O,.

my

my God! fhall my refurrection be equally
fatal to me?—Have pity on my calamities!
—Shall I offend thee by haftening a period
whofe approach I already feel? But I fhall
be exempted from forrow, from ignominy.
——My God, if I have incurred thy wrath,
am I not already fufficiently punifhed?—
Death is the only bleffing thou haft in
ftore for me; and I accept it.——Now
will I throw myfelf down.—But my fon!—
who will fupply the place of a mother to
him?"—

After a fhort paufe, fhe thus proceeded,
with a wildnefs yet more gloomy.

" Why fhould he not plunge into the
arms of Death with me?—Of what avail is
life, when it is confumed by grief, when it
is ftained by difgrace and meannefs, when
it is dependent for its fcanty fupport upon
the infulting aid of pity?—Ah! my fon, is
it thus that we ought to exift?——Ought

this

this to be the fate of the blood of the earl of Somerfet ?——Muft not thou die as well as thy unhappy mother ?—Alas ! thou wilt reproach me for having given birth to thee.—— We are two wretches connected to each other by Adverfity yet more powerfully than by Nature.——Let us perifh then together."——

And fhe flew to the child, in order to execute her dreadful purpofe. The little innocent fcreamed with terror, and eagerly clafped his mother ; who, turning her eyes upon him, and fhedding a torrent of tears, exclaimed " No, my dear child," I will not take away thy life; I will not deftroy the all that remains to me of my dear Belford.—Go ;— I will water thee with my tears, I will feed thee with my very heart. —Thou fhalt live—live to lament and to love me.—Great God ! let his misfortunes



be

be one day mitigated, and let me fuffer with my laſt figh !"——

Having embraced her ſon, ſhe again threw herſelf before the tomb. Alarmed by the groans of a perſon who ſeemed to be in the agonies of death, ſhe attempted to fly from this place of horror. The groans en-creaſed ; and her fear gave way to her com-paſſion. She advanced toward the ſpot from whence the inarticulate ſounds ſeem-ed to proceed; and ſhe beheld a man ſtretched upon a tomb-ſtone, with his hands upon his face, and almoſt without breath. Prompted by pity, ſhe flew to a brook at a little diſtance for ſome water, in order to recall the ſtranger to life. He recovered his ſenſes, in ſome meaſure, and raiſed his head.——What were the ſenſations of Lady Harriet, when ſhe found that the objeÖt of her benevolence was Rich-ard, the ſon of her worthy benefaÖtor,

the

the favage Richard, who had murdered her hufband by his oppreffions, and who had barbaroufly turned herfelf and her babe out of the farm !

" Ah !" cried Richard, with a faltering voice, expreffive of the moft bitter diftrefs," " is it to thee that I am indebted for this relief ? —The vengeance of heaven would have been incomplete without this ftroke. ——To receive this generous affiftance from the perfon I treated with the greateft cruelty !——If thou hadft any thing for me to eat !—I have not tafted food for upwards of two days :—I am almoft fpeechlefs with hunger."—

Lady Harriet, whofe compaffion could only be exceeded by her aftonifhment, immediately divided in two a morfel of bread which fhe had intended for her child.

" Art

" Art thou, Richard," faid fhe, " reduced to this extremity ?—Here—I forget all
the diftrefs thou haft brought upon me——
fhare with my child this bit of bread.—
It is the only relief which my deplorable fituation enables me to afford to thee.———
Behold, Richard, the effects of thy cruelty!
———But by what accident haft thou been
plunged into this abyfs of mifery ?—How I
fympathife with thee, and how forry I am
that I cannot ferve thee !———I fhould be
glad to acquit myfelf of the obligations I
owe to thy father."—

" My father," replied Richard, fo foon
as he had devoured his morfel, " foretold to
me that heaven would punifh me for my
want of humanity ;——heaven, which now
loads me with all the feverity of its juftice,
which avenges Belford, which avenges thee.
—It was Avarice which taught me to be
cruel. In contempt of the duties of Religion,

gion and of Nature, I endeavoured to enrich myfelf by unlawful means. My difhonefty was detected; my farm was taken from me; and I was forced to make my efcape, in order to avoid the horrors of a gaol. Thefe, however, were not my only difafters. A gang of robbers ftripped me of the little all which remained to me;———of all but thefe rags which cover me.—Shut out from every avenue to relief, afraid of punifhment from Man, torn with remorfe, and ready to finifh my days without the hope of obtaining my pardon from Heaven, which I have offended too heinoufly, I have received from thee, whom I oppreffed with unexampled barbarity, from thee, who fhouldft rejoice at my fad fate, that relief which not another being upon earth would think himfelf bound to beftow upon me.———Generous woman !— If God hears the prayers of the wicked, thy virtues will be rewarded.——— My punifh- ment will then feem lefs terrible."———

Lady

Lady Harriet interrupted him with her tears.

" The only favour I have to beg," continued Richard, " is, that thou wilt pardon me, that thou wilt interceed for me with heaven, which I have wearied out with my crimes.—I am thankful that it has not denied me the comfort of expiring in thy fight."——

Lady Harriet difcovered the utmoft fenfibility for the terrible fituation of Richard; who now, whether from defpair, or whether what he had eaten had been prejudicial to him after fo long a faft, funk into another fwoon, and foon after yielded up his laft breath with heaven and his benefactrefs upon his lips.

The terrified Lady Harriet haftened from this fcene of death. Providence feemed willing to confole her, by fhewing her a

dreadful

dreadful picture of his vengeance in the tragical end of her perfecutor. Yet that incomprehenfible wifdom, which punifhes the guilty, and which protects the virtuous, permitted not the fate of Lady Harriet to be changed, or in the fmalleft degree foftened. She drank of the cup of forrow to the very dregs; fhe was oppreffed with humiliation; and fhe experienced all that anguifh of foul which is infeparable from mifery, when it is degraded to the pitch of foliciting that fluggifh compaffion whofe every favour is an infult.

Often did fhe fay to herfelf, " My God, wilt thou not forgive me?—Shall I die with the curfe of a father upon me?—What an exiftence, my fon, have I given to thee!—If Lord Somerfet did but fee thee, he would melt at thy tears;—he would open to thee that bofom which he has fhut againft me.— Yes, he would melt;——he would no longer be able to with-hold from me his pardon;

don;

don;—he would deign to receive my expiring foul."——

It was by a miracle of maternal love that this unhappy creature had been enabled to fupport life fo long. Shunning the towns, fhe crawled from village to village; and at laft, rejected at every quarter, and quite fpent under the burthen of her diftrefs, fhe was ready to perifh with want and with difeafe. Only one poor woman, who herfelf craved the charity of the public, took pity on her fituation, and received her into a ftable, which afforded her a nightly fhelter from the weather.—The daughter of Lord Somerfet was now, amidft the agonies of death, ftretched upon a bed of ftraw.——Her ftrength was totally exhaufted; fhe was fpeechlefs; her eyes were two fountains of tears.——She gazed upon her child, embraced him, and fell into a fwoon;—— her child, who feemed to fhare the diftrefs

of

of his mother, who mingled his tears and his groans with hers.——What a picture of diſtreſs !————Can there be on earth beings ſo wretched, ſo abandoned by ſociety, whoſe cries daily pierce our ears, who endeavour to force their tears into our very hearts, and whom yet, inſtead of relieving, we hardly beſtow a ſingle look at ?——

Lady Harriet, as the laſt effort of affection for her ſon, determined to write to her father once more. She could not think of death, till ſhe knew into whoſe hands her ſon ſhould fall. She begged a bit of paper and ſome ink from the woman, who, ignorant of her rank, had relieved her merely from an impulſe of humanity.————As Harriet took up the paper, her tears flowed yet more faſt.

" My dear benefactreſs," ſaid ſhe, " I have not been always thus.————You little

think

think that you have obliged the daughter of a peer."————

" The daughter of a peer !" exclaimed the aftonifhed woman—" Alas ! madam, would I had it in my power to do you a greater fervice !——You know my own dif-trefs."——

" I know thy generofity, the greatnefs' of thy foul," replied Lady Harriet.——" When every heart upon earth feemed to have become callous to me, thine bled for my diftreffes.—Yes, my dear friend—how truly doft thou deferve that title !——yes, I am the daughter of a peer ; and I die with no other fupport but what I owe to thy cha-rity."—

"Charity!"--At that word, her voice became inarticulate with fobs.—On her recovery, fhe took up the pen, and difpatched a long letter to
her

her father, blotted with tears. She enlarged upon the affection she bore, upon the duty she owed, to him; upon her errors, her repentance, the fatal confequences of her mifconduct, the lofs of her hufband, the adverfity which had overwhelmed him, and the mifery into which herfelf was plunged. She conjured him, in the name of Nature and of Humanity, to relieve her from the weight of his malediction, to receive her laft fighs; and she concluded with intreating, that he would reftore the worthy Dr. Willis, whofe generofity she never fhould forget, to that favour which he had forfeited by ferving her; and that he would extend his protection and bounty to the charitable woman, who alone had interefted herfelf in her diftrefs. In a poftfcript she added,

" Make hafte, my lord—I dare not call you father—and clofe the eyes of—fhall I fay it?—your unhappy daughter.——Deny

me

me not a name, which I shall soon relin-
quish for ever.—My soul longs to expire in
your bosom——in the bosom of a parent,
who, at this moment, is more dear to me
than ever.——Can he still refuse to me his
pardon?——Oh! grant it, my lord, grant
it, for the sake of a little innocent, whom
I throw at your feet, who stretches out his
hands to you as an intercession for his mother.———My lord—my father, suffer me
to die in your embrace.—If I have offended
you, come to witness the punishment I
suffer. I dare not believe that your wrath
can extend further.——Once more deign to
yield to my entreaties, to my tears.—Come,
and let my last looks be divided between
you and my child!"

The benevolent woman, who had not yet
recovered from her astonishment, undertook
to forward the letter by a special messenger.

"I

" I imagined," said she to Lady Harriet, " from the refpect with which you infpired me, that your birth muft have been widely different from mine."——

" Ah ! my worthy, my only friend," in_terrupted the other, " let us not talk of re-fpect.—Refpect belongs not to me.——In my prefent condition, it is fufficient that I have moved thy compaffion.——Thy fenfibility commands refpect.——My father will requite the uncommon obligations I owe to thee.——At fight of my letter his refent-ment will furely be difarmed !——My dear child," continued she, taking her fon in her arms, " I ftill truft that thou wilt be a ftranger to the misfortunes of thy mother.——My lord will not abandon thee !—— No: thou wilt find in him a protector, a father."—

The

The lofs of his daughter was ftill frefh in the memory of the earl ; and fhe ceafed not to engrofs the whole of his converfation with Doctor Willis. He would have preferred the moft abject poverty to all the pomp and fplendour with which he was furrounded, if with that poverty he could have recovered his Harriet.———Religion was now his only fupport ; and the doctor, who could not himfelf refrain from fhedding a tear at the name of Lady Harriet, exerted every effort to confole him.

The meffenger, on his arrival, immediately defired to fpeak with the earl ; and he delivered the letter into his own hand.——— His lordfhip had hardly opened it, when he funk into a fwoon ; and, as he recovered from it, " My daughter, my daughter !" cried he, " into what an abyfs art thou plunged !———Come, Willis, let us fet off ;— let me fee, let me embrace her, let me convince

vince her, that I am ſtill the tendereſt of fathers.—Should I loſe her !—She has not forgotten thy kindneſs, doctor.—Oh ! heaven, heaven, reſtore to me my daughter !—her ſon—he is mine—he is my ſon—I am the moſt criminal of men."——

It is not in language to expreſs the diſtraction of Lord Somerſet.—He aſked an hundred queſtions of the meſſenger about the ſituation of his daughter ; and when her deplorable retreat was mentioned, he fell back as if thunderſtruck, ſcreaming out, " Is my Harriet, my Harriet, reduced to this extremity ?"—

It was not long before his lordſhip, eager to ſnatch his daughter from deſtruction, was in readineſs for his journey. The worthy paſtor accompanied him.—Every now and then he exclaimed with a ſigh, " Is it poſſible that I ſhould have brought down this

diſtreſs

diſtreſs upon my child ?——that I, her father, ſhould have plunged her into this
gulph of wretchedneſs ?"——

He was now fully convinced of the
treachery of his ſiſter.

" Alas !" continued he, " if the former letter had not been intercepted, it might not,
even now perhaps, have been too late to
have reſtored my dear Harriet to happineſs.—Ah ! ſhould ſhe be torn from me—
ſhould I find her expiring—ſhould ſhe be
no longer able to receive my embraces, my
tears !——Willis, I would not ſurvive the
ſtroke :——there is no puniſhment which I
ought not to undergo."——

The earl flew towards the wretched
manſion of his daughter——His whole
ſoul darted into her arms. Already did he
enjoy the pleaſure of embracing her, of

em-

imploring her forgivenefs.——What tranfports are there to compare with thofe of paternal love ?

The impatience of Lady Harriet to behold her father was equally great.

" Surely," faid fhe, " my father will not
be fo relentlefs as to deny me the comfort
of feeing him !——No :——I fhall carry his
bleffing with me to the grave——he will
have pity upon my child !"——

And fhe preffed the lovely innocent to her
bofom.

Fortune had not yet exhaufted all her
fury upon this unhappy creature. From one
fainting fit fhe fell into another, till at
length—how dreadful was the thought !——
how many deaths did it convey to her !—
fhe began to fear that her father would not

arrive in time to receive her laſt ſigh.——
Yet with tears and ſighs ſhe ceaſed not to
ſolicit heaven for this ſingle favour.


" O my God!" did ſhe often repeat,
" my God! permit me to fix my eyes upon
thoſe of my father !—permit me to tell him,
that I die begging his pardon, loving him !
—that I recommend to him my ſon !—permit my heart to beat, once more, under his
paternal hand, and then take from me this
breath, this remnant, of a wretched life !"—


The worthy woman, who was by her
ſide, endeavoured, with every argument
of which ſhe was miſtreſs, to diſpel her
grief, which yet became more and more
alarming. Convinced of the near approach
of death, and without a hope of ſeeing her
father, Harriet begged that her friend would
ſupport her, while, with a trembling hand,

ſhe

fhe wrote the following letter to his lordfhip :

" Death, my father, hangs over me,
ready to clofe my eyes, and yet I have not
feen thee !——Yes, my lord, every thing
tells me, that I fhall not have the fatisfaction of receiving thee into my arms, of receiving thy blefling.——It was the only favour I afked of heaven—and I am denied
it.——I feel that I fhall expire without
weeping upon thy hands, without calling
thee father.——Love, love, my lord, is
the fource of my guilt, the fource of all
my misfortunes.——What an awful leffon to the youth of my fex !——But are
not heaven and thou fufficiently revenged ?—Thy daughter, my lord, the daughter of the earl of Somerfet, hath wandered
over the fields for charity; and fhe now dies
in a ftable.—Whom has fhe to comfort her ?—
a woman, who is herfelf moft wretched, who,

like

like thy Harriet, depends for her fupport upon
the bounty of the public.——She, my lord, is
my only friend.———On her wretched bofom
my dying head fhall fall ;———from her thou
wilt receive my breathlefs body, my unhappy child.————Reject him not, my lord.
He has the heart of his mother——he will
be obedient to thee—he will love thee.——I
die with this laft hope, that he will endeavour to atone for my faults.—In the grave
I fhall feel every carefs thou beftoweft upon
him, every tear thou fheddeft over him.——
Deny not to my fad remains that benedic-
tion which I could not obtain when alive.
—Let thy tears flow—— alas ! mine fhall
be dried up.——I fhall be incapable of pro-
ftrating myfelf at thy feet —thy daughter
fhall be no more.———Horrid idea to die
thus !—


" Vouchfafe, I intreat thee once more,
to remember my benefactor, the worthy
Doctor

Doctor Willis, and to reward as she deferves, the only being upon earth who has endeavoured to alleviate my diftrefs.——Adieu, my father!—My father!—with my whole foul do I pronounce that name.——Shed a tear to my memory, and love me in my child."

Lady Harriet defired that this letter might be put into her hand, and that it fhould be expofed thus to the view of her father, if fhe fhould expire before his arrival.———— Fortune ceafed not to frown upon her to the laft moment.——She died, embracing her fon—died, without having the comfort of even beholding the author of her days.

Her requeft was faithfully complied with, while the weeping child threw himfelf upon the body of his mother, who feemed ftill to ftretch out her hands to him.

" Where

" Where, where is my daughter ?" cried the earl, rushing in, attended by Willis and the messenger.—" In what a situation !—she is no more !—her child—my dear son !" were the incoherent exclamations of the distracted father.————He embraced his daughter and the child, while he rent the air with his cries.————The letter rendered him yet more desperate.————He could not tear himself from the body, which he clasped in his arms, constantly repeating, " My daughter, my dear daughter, to this art thou reduced by my barbarity !" and he would instantly have destroyed himself, if Doctor Willis, who was not an unconcerned spectator of this scene, had not soothed him with the dictates of religion, which alone could enable him to support such complicated distress. At length they prevailed upon him to retire. Long did he remain in a stupor of grief; nor did he recover from it but to devote the remainder of

his

his days to piety, and to the fuperinten-
dance of the education of his grandfon, who
inherited his name, his titles and his fortune. On the bed of death he charged Dr.
Willis to refide with the youth, as a friend;
and it is almoft needlefs to add, that he raifed to independence the woman who had fo
generoufly relieved his daughter.

. The young lord ceafed not to revere the
memory of his grandfather, ceafed not to
love, with all the affection of a fon, the venerable Dr. Willis, who died at an advanced age.———He efpoufed a young lady,
who had been long the victim of adverfity,
in preference to one of the moft opulent
heireffes in the kingdom; for his mother, who
perpetually engroffed his thoughts, had en-
deared to him the title of Unfortunate.
Upon the fpot where fhe expired he founded
an hofpital; and thither he repaired every
year, in order to pafs a month in relieving
the diftreffes of the poor.

" My

" My friends," faid he often to them, " ye are my brethren.—Thus my mother lived, thus fhe died ;——I refpect and cherifh her in you.——May the care I take of you, and the tears I fhed to her memory, reach to her even in the grave !——O, my mother, it is to thee that I am indebted for this fenfibility, which is the pride of my foul !———why canft thou not reap the fruits of it ?"—

In the centre of this hofpital, his lordfhip erected a ftatue in remembrance of the unfortunate Lady Harriet.—Often did he retire to embrace it, and to weep at the foot of it.— He died a model of virtue and of benevolence; qualities which have immortalized him in the hearts of his countrymen.

# ROSETTA:

## OR, THE

## FAIR PENITENT REWARDED.

# ROSETTA:

## OR, THE

## FAIR PENITENT REWARDED.

NEXT to Virtue itſelf, that unvaried object of our homage, what ought, above
all things, to command the eſteem of the
world, to excite in us an eſteem for ourſelves,
is the return to Virtue, from whoſe paths
there are few, who, at one period or another, do not deviate. True repentance, by
working upon our ſenſibility, renders our
morals, in ſome meaſure, more pure, and

helps,

helps to eradicate from our hearts that vanity, which is almoſt inſeparable from thoſe who have never ſwerved from their duty. Self-love, bold as the expreſſion may appear, though it is nearly a kin to virtue, is yet the moſt formidable enemy which it has to encounter. They who have once experienced the frailty of their nature, will be confident without pride, will be humble amidſt every advantage. The wiſh to atone for their tranſgreſſions will give ſtrength to their reſolution, and the fear of a relapſe will not permit them to triumph.——Beſides, let us liſten to the dictates of Religion and of Wiſdom.——Do not theſe inform us, that real penitence is an infallible title to the pardon of heaven?—And ſhall man be more rigid than the deity?— ſhall he forget that lenity and compaſſion are the grand attributes of his being, that, without them, Virtue is but a name?——— Let us liſten to thoſe of Nature, which guides us to Truth, as it were,

by

by the hand, and which eternally calls upon us to open our hearts to the fighs of the unhappy.——The unhappy !—Can there be any beings that are more fo, any that are more deferving of our utmoft confolation and tendernefs, than thofe, who, impreffed with an eternal forrow for their deviation from virtue, return to it with tears, and feel, that, without it, there is no happinefs.

Such were my reflections, vague as they may, at the firft glance, appear, upon the perufal of the two following letters, from which I claim no other merit than that of prefenting them to the public. I imagined that they might throw a new light upon what is generally termed " Morality," that they might fix our ideas with regard to virtue, and the rank it ought to hold in the hearts of thofe who are capable to withftand prejudice, and to yield to truth ;——truth,

which,

which, though it is the moſt important ſtudy of man, is yet almoſt univerſally neglected by him as unworthy of his attention.

## From Sir HENRY LENOX to CHARLES NEWBURGH, *Eſq.*

THOU art my friend, Charles:—I know it.———Attend, therefore, and pronounce my future happineſs or miſery. I now ſend to thee my ſoul : in return for which, exert thine to guide me, to enlighten me ; in a word, to determine my deſtiny.———Charles, I am in love—in love, to a degree I never felt till now. I am myſelf aſtoniſhed at it. —Yet blame me not till thou haſt heard my ſtory.

Thou knoweſt how fond Lord Villars and I are of long walks—walks, which, to thee, my friend, would appear as ſo many journies. His lordſhip inſiſts, that ſuch exerciſes

cifes are no lefs falutary to the mind than
to the body ;—infifts, that we cannot mul-
tiply too many objects before us, and
that by thefe means——allow me the meta-
phor—we are fupplied with provifions toward a fund of philofophy, which is the
conftant nourifhment of every being who
knows the value of his exiftence.—Villars
feems to have penetrated into the very re-
ceffes of Nature. Nothing efcapes his notice. For an hour will he reafon—reafon
with all the depth of the moft fkilful natu-
ralift—upon a flower of the field, which any
other but himfelf would have trampled under foot.—His converfation, which is wholely fentimental, excites and cherifhes in the
foul a certain delicacy, a certain tendernefs,
which feem to pave a paffage for the impreffions of love. I hardly need to tell thee of
my fenfibility, or of the unhappy iffue of
my paffion for Mifs Howard ;——Mifs
Howard, whofe perfidy can only be equalled

by

by her charms.——No more of her.——Her empire, my friend, is at an end.——I have already done homage at another shrine.—— Surely all women are not hypocrites.

Our philosopher and I, during one of our excursions, advanced insensibly toward a farm-house, the situation of which charmed us.——The avenue to it was lined with oaks ; and, at a little distance from it, there was a valley enamelled with the gayest verdure, through which flowed a rivulet that disappeared amidst an orchard of apple-trees. The adjacent declivities were covered with sheep; the beams of the sun sparkled through a thicket of trees, which, as if proud of their antiquity, out-towered a hill that sheltered this delightful spot from the north wind ; and a village, rendered beautiful by the varied structure of its buildings, closed the delightful landscape.

By

By a kind of involuntary impulfe, we entered the houfe, where we were received with a fmile of hofpitality unknown to the buftling fons of commerce or of diffipation. The farmer, a venerable old man, immediately covered for us his humble board, and laid before us fome milk, fome butter, and a few eggs. We accepted his invitation with thanks; and as we rofe to take our leave, Villars attempted to put a piece of gold into his hand. He looked as if we had intended an affront to him. I perceived it; and, taking off a gold ring, of no great value, which I had upon my finger, I put it upon that of his daughter.

We had not proceeded many fteps when we came to a rivulet, by the fide of which fat a girl who tended a few fheep. My eyes had no fooner met thofe of Rofetta—fo the lovely ruftic was called —than my whole frame was in a commotion, my every fenfe was engroffed by the charming object before me.—Form to thyfelf two large black eyes, fraught with expreffion, a fhape modelled by elegance, the graces of nature in their full difplay, the bloom of youth, an air of fenfibility and languor——form to thyfelf the image of Love, my friend, and thou haft Rofetta before thee.——Thou wilt be amazed when I tell thee that fhe had a book in her hand. At our approach fhe thruft it into her pocket.—I advanced to her, and fhe fpoke. My aftonifhment encreafed at the found of her voice. Though the few words fhe uttered were merely thofe of civility, they yet convinced me that the foul of Rofetta was fuperior to her condition ; nor did Villars differ from me in that opinion.

Rofetta engroffed our converfation the whole day.—At night I felt, that the ideas, or rather the feelings, with which the fair fhepherdefs had infpired me, were rooted in

my

my heart—felt, that I was once more in-
tangled in the toils of love. I determined,
however, to conceal my fentiments from
Villars. The next day he marked my
thoughtful filence, and afked the caufe of it.
I fatisfied him, though not with the truth.
—There are fecrets in love which are in-
violable even to a friend.——In the after-
noon, I efcaped from his lordfhip, and flew
to the fpot where I had feen Rofetta.

I found her in the very pofture in which
we had beheld her the day before. The
fame book was in her hand, and the fentiments with which it feemed to imprefs her,
yet heightened her charms.

" Start not," faid I to her as I advanced ;
" —ftart not, my lovely girl, at feeing me
again."——

She

She could not conceal from me her confufion.


" I have been a ftranger to happinefs fince
I parted 'from thee.——Wilt thou fo far indulge my curiofity, as to inform me by what
miracle thou wert brought to this fpot, wert
reduced to this fituation.———Thou canft
not difguife from me thy rank.—No : my
heart tells me that there are few who deferve
thee."——


" Deferve me !" interrupted Rofetta,
with a face crimfoned with blufhes——-
" Alas ! Sir, my rank is no wife fuperior to that in which you fee me.——
Fortune owes nothing to me.———Would
I had always lived in this unknown retreat !
—It is the manfion of Virtue, and"—with
a figh fhe added—" it muft be that of Happinefs."—


A tear

A tear forced itself into her bosom.

" Thou weepest !—I will not urge thee to explain thy story.——Yet, believe me, thou hast captivated a heart which shall be thine through life."——

Ought I to repeat to thee our converfation? —My friend, I could not.—Suffice it, that it clofed not but with the day, that fhe told me her name, that I felt myfelf yet more enraptured.—Clariffa, the glory of the immortal Richardfon, was the book which fhe had been reading.

Though Rofetta fcrupled not to tell me her name, though her every motion pronounced her unformed for the employment in which fhe was engaged, fhe yet with-held from me the fecret of her birth.

Every

Every day did I fee the miftrefs of my heart, every day did fhe chain me to her by a new rivet.—I hear thee exclaim, "What a fool, to treat with fo much ceremony a fimple peafant!"——Charles, thou haft not feen the divine Rofetta, haft not heard her voice.——I ventured to declare to her my paffion.—Give ear to her anfwer.——It is Rofetta who fpeaks——Rofetta, whofe every word finks too deep into the heart not to leave a lafting impreffion.

"Were it in my power, Sir, I freely confefs that I would not hefitate to yield to you my heart, in return for that affection with which you have honoured me;—an affection which, I am willing to believe, has virtue and efteem for its bafis.——Yet let me conjure you to banifh me from your thoughts.——May I be enabled to think no more of you!——I can never be your wife, or the wife of any man.—Leave me there-

fore

fore to that forrow which death alone can terminate ; and perfift not—if I have any title to the regard which you exprefs for me—perfift not to enquire into the fate of an unhappy creature whom"—and a flood of tears burft from her eyes——" whom you would defpife, were you acquainted with her ftory."—

" Defpife thee, Rofetta ! No : rather fay thou wilt not receive the adoration I pay to thee.——The purity, the warmth, of my love for thee are not to be expreffed.—Each day I fee thee, I behold in thee new charms. --Tell me by what facrifice I may render thee mine.—" Thy ftory !"—My Rofetta is unhappy, and fhe yet will not fuffer me to enjoy the tranfport of flying to her relief !"—

" Relief !——No, Sir," interrupted fhe with warmth, " you can only heighten my diftrefs.——Compel me not, I again be-
feech

feech you, to tell you what I would rather die than divulge.——Shall I find in you an enemy, a tormentor ?"—

" No, Rofetta, thou fhalt not.——I will obey thee implicitly.——I will never more fpeak to thee of my love."——

Thefe words brought tears from my heart;—tears, which feemed to melt the foul of Rofetta.

I continued to fee my charmer every day. Yet, enflaved to her will, I no longer told her the wifhes of my heart.—I riveted my eyes upon her, and fighed in filence.—— At every interview I found, that my love, my friendfhip, for her encreafed——found, that her underftanding, though exalted, was yet inferior to the fenfibility, the benevolence, the generofity, which animated her heart. I dared not, becaufe I truly loved ——— and they who truly love are fearful of giving offence.—I dared not to confide my fecret with the worthy people with whom fhe lived. This reſtraint had nearly proved fatal to me. From the bed of ſickneſs I wrote to Rofetta the agony of mind and of body under which I laboured ; and fhe came to fee me, accompanied by one of her maſter's daughters, the fame to whom I had preſented the ring.———The preſence of an angel from heaven could hardly have excited in me greater joy.——Never did fhe appear more beautiful, more powerfully furrounded with the inexpreſſible, the bewitching, charms of love.

In attempting to addreſs me, fhe burſt into tears.

" Behold, cruel, yet dear Rofetta," I cried, " to what a fituation thou haſt reduced me !"—

" I do

" I do behold it, Sir—behold it, and confefs that it diftracts me.——At the expence
of my life would I purchafe thy felicity.—
But thou fhalt hear my ftory, and from that
determine  my doom and your own—determine whether my heart  ought again to admit the impreffions of love."—

She could not proceed for fobs.

" I am about to facrifice to  thee my vanity, my fecret,  about to plunge myfelf into forrow, into fhame, and into difgrace—
about  to render myfelf odious to the man
whofe efteem I ought above all  things  to
endeavour to preferve.————What wouldft
thou have of  me ?"——

" Thy hand, Rofetta.—Permit me to enjoy the happinefs  of adoring thee throughout my life."——

" Hap-

" Happinefs !—Alas, Sir, it is not in my power to render either thee or myfelf happy.—Know then my every forrow ;—know—Ah! cruel man, why doft thou compel me to open afrefh my wounds—to pour forth to thee the fecrets of a heart, which, tho' it can never be thine, fhall yet not ceafe to love thee."

She looked as if her heart would burft.

" Am I, Rofetta," I cried, taking her by the hand, " am I the caufe of thefe convulvulfive fobs ?—Sooner would I fuffer a thoufand deaths than excite in thy bofom one fenfation of forrow.————No : I will not force from thee the ftory of thy woes ; and ——if it muft be fo—never let us fee each other more.————When thou heareft of my diftrefs, wilt thou pity me ?"————

" Pity thee !—Alas ! Sir, why wilt thou love, efteem, an object that is unworthy of

the

thy notice ?—Since it muſt be ſo, I will tell thee all.--Emily," continu'd ſhe, looking tenderly at the young woman who accompanied her, " mingle thy tears with mine——let me not forfeit thy friendſhip by what I ſhall now reveal.—I have no ſecret which ought to be concealed from thee."—And turning to me with a ſigh, " After this explanation, I ſhall never ſee thee again, ſpeak to thee, unfold to thee a heart which—which is full of thee.——To make an offer to me of thy love then, would be to inſult me ; to add to that offer thy hand, would be an honour of which I feel the utmoſt value, but which I can never deſerve.—

" I bluſh not at my birth. I owe it to parents, who, though poor farmers in the county of Devonſhire, had yet wealth ſufficient to procure for me an education ſuperior to my condition. An increaſe of knowledge is frequently attended with an increaſe

of vanity; and to this proof of their affection I may, perhaps, afcribe my ruin. The
happinefs, the very exiftence, of my father,
who was advanced in years before I was
born, and of my mother, depended upon
me. My every word and action feemed to
promife, that I fhould be a fupport to them
in their old age, a comfort to them in the
hour of death, and an honour to their memory.

" How often have they held me in their
arms, and faid to me with tears, Rofetta,
thou dear pledge of our love, we leave to
thee little wealth, but we leave to thee our
example to follow, the example of a family
who, from father to fon, have for two hundred years, like us, laboured thefe fields.
They were proud of the plough, whofe chief
inheritance is virtue;—virtue which—and
we charge thee never to forget it—is the only fource of happinefs on earth.———Exult

in

in thy poverty while it is honeſt.—Continue to live in this village;——die in it, and be buried beſide us.—Go not to London:—the inhabitants of the town are full of vice, and will corrupt thee.——Do as we have done, and have thy maker perpetually in thy eye.—

" My maker !—And I have already renounced him—have renounced the dictates of honour, of duty, of nature—have lived to ſtain the memory of the dear, the venerable, authors of my being."

At theſe words, ſpeechleſs with tears, ſhe ſat before me, the living picture of grief.

" Ah ! Roſetta," cried I, preſſing her hand with eagerneſs, " poſſeſſed of theſe ſentiments, thou art ſtill the moſt valuable, the moſt adorable, of women.——Pour out thy tears, thy ſoul, into my boſom, into the

boſom

bofom of a faithful friend, who will partake
of thy forrows."————

Thus fhe proceeded with a look of anguifh which pierced me.

" I had fome beauty————perhaps I was
not ignorant that I had it—and was endued
with all the charms of innocence, with a
heart that, unhappily, was open to every impreffion of tendernefs, when my cruel deftiny brought into our neighbourhood, and prefented to my view, the moft amiable—the
moft abandoned of men.   Befides the graces
of figure, he poffeffed thofe appendages which
are fo apt to captivate the heart of woman,
titles, wealth and fplendour—poffeffed the
whole artillery of feduction.————What a
powerful enemy for an inexperienced girl
to combat!—I refifted, at times I even fuppreffed, thofe feelings which had like to have
enflaved me.   Perpetually did I call to re-
mem-

membrance, that I was only the daughter of a peasant, that I ought not to
encourage a single thought about Lord
Darnley."————

"Lord Darnley! is that wretch, Rosetta,
the author of thy distress?—I know him to
have been the very scourge of virtue; and at
length he hath received the reward of his
crimes.—Two months have not elapsed since
he fell in a duel in Germany."—

" Then he is no more!" exclaimed she,
raising her eyes to heaven.

And she paused.

" May a blessed repentance have opened
his eyes!—May the vengeance of heaven
pursue him not beyond the grave!——Yes,
Sir, Lord Darnley was the author of all my
sorrows, of my eternal despair.  He introduced

duced himself to my parents, I forget upon what pretence, though his motive was, to accomplish my ruin, which he had planned from the moment he first beheld me. As he frequently renewed his visits to our cottage, he soon found an opportunity to direct a few words to me;———words, whose subtle poison, like a rapid flame, darted to my heart. He wrote to me; and I had not resolution to reject a letter which gave the fatal blow to my enfeebled virtue. Regardless of my duty, of my honour, I was so weak as to appoint an interview with the faithless Darnley. Then, giving full scope to his villany, did he throw himself at my feet, water them with his tears, vow that he longed to call me his, and that, if I would go with him to London, our wedding should there be solemnized. He painted to me the most brilliant scenes which Pleasure, Wealth and Grandeur can exhibit; and he concluded with an entreaty, that I would keep our secret inviolate, that I would tear myſelf from the boſom of parental tenderneſs, without mentioning either my intention or the place of my retreat.

" I loved, and I had already ſtifled every ſentiment of virtue. Nature, however, ſtill retained her influence. The idea of abandoning my father and mother, without informing them of at leaſt the cauſe of our ſeparation, ſhocked me. Darnley perceived that it did—perceived, that filial duty was too ſtrong for love. He drew his ſword as if he would, that inſtant, have thruſt it into his heart. I trembled for his life, and held him.———My fooliſh tenderneſs prevailed, and——I promiſed an implicit compliance with his requeſt.

What were the ſtruggles, what was the torture, which I experienced during the eve of my elopement !—Never had the tenderneſs

nefs of my father and mother melted me fo before. I ftemmed floods of tears, which would have forced a paffage from my very heart at the thought of parting from parents fo indulgent, of depriving them, in their old age, of their only comfort, their only prop.——

" Dear Rofetta," faid my father to me, " doft thou feel how neceffary thou art to our happinefs ?—For thee alone do I culti-vate thofe fields, do I water them, at thefe years, with my fweat.——My child, I now dig for myfelf a grave——ere long thou wilt clofe my eyes."—

At thefe words, my weeping mother clafped me with one arm to her heart, while fhe ftretched out the other to my father.

" Oh ! my dear parents," cried I, throw-ing myfelf before them, " I have"——

And

And at that inftant, when the fecret qui-
vered upon my lips, did Darnley enter. He
darted at me a look ;—and I again wavered
between nature and love. Unable to withftand the dreadful conflict, I fell into a
fwoon. I was put to bed ; and on opening
my eyes in the morning, I found myfelf in
a poft-chaife, with Darnley by my fide, and
above twenty miles from home. The fervants of this perfidious lord, as I have been
fince informed, had procured accefs to my
apartment in the dead of the night, and
had carried me, ftill lifelefs, into the arms
of their mafter, whofe carriage waited to
receive us.—

What were my fenfations when I awaked!
——I found myfelf unable to return to the
bofom of my parents. I loft fight of virtue ;
——loft fight of every thing but love and
the corrupter of my innocence, whom I then
beheld in a very different light. On our
arrival in London, I contented myfelf with
weeping

weeping for my parents, with cherifhing the remembrance of them ; and at length, upon the promife of a marriage, which from day to day he ftill found means to evade; I re-figned myfelf a victim to the treachery of Lord Darnley.

Fortune heaped upon me her gifts. I was furrounded with pleafure, — furrounded with admirers, who fomented in me that fort of intoxication into which his lordfhip wifhed to plunge me. But when my eyes withdrew from thefe delufions, when I look-ed into my heart, what a fight prefented it-felf!—Then did I hear the groans of affli-&ed nature, did I behold the image of an unhappy father and mother, weeping for their loft, their difhonoured daughter, and re-calling her to her duty with all the ten-dernefs, all the anguifh, of parental affection. What a dreadful fituation!—How unavailing

is wealth, when unaccompanied with innocence !—Sometimes I refolved to fly back to
my parents; but the buftle of a vicious
world deftroyed thefe happy emotions, and
ftupefied me under the load of a grief which
confumed me.

One evening Darnley, with a numerous
company, carried me to the play-houfe. I
forget the title of the piece. In one fcene
there appeared a grey-haired old man, with
a mattock in his hand, the picture of venerable poverty, who faid to a young woman
loaded with diamonds, " Ah ! my daughter, I fee thy wealth—where is thy virtue ?"--

I fcreamed out, " Oh ! my father!" and
fainted away.

I was told, that the whole audience had
heard my cry. On opening my eyes, I
found myfelf in his lordfhip's houfe, furrounded

rounded by fome of his vifitors, who were endeavouring to recall me to life.—I fprung from their arms, and threw myfelf, all pale and difhevelled, at Darnley's feet.

" My lord," I cried to him, " I have heard my doom, my duty, at the theatre.—Have pity on an unhappy girl; and, in return for her love, reftore to her her honour.——Suffer me once more to behold my parents, to be honoured by their poverty.—Suffer me to retire into their cottage, to die in it, as thy wife.—I claim not from thy generofity, thy humanity, either titles or wealth:—I claim, let me repeat it, the name, the name alone, of wife.—Thou fhalt not have caufe to be afhamed of me," I added, clafping his knees." " With that name let me enjoy one day of tears with my parents, and then bury me in fome unknown retreat, throw me into a dungeon, ftab me, kill me;—and I will blefs thee.—

Reflect,

Reflect, my lord, that it was upon thy pro-
mise of acknowledging me for thy wife,
that I was seduced, ruined.——Wouldst
thou abuse the credulity of an unfortunate
creature, who hath not upon earth a friend
but thee?"——

The company, unable to contain their
tears, withdrew. The servants still remained, to witness the villany of the monster
in its full display.

" Whence," he cried, with eyes sparkling
with rage; " whence proceeds this infolence?—Was it at the play you learned
these fine sentiments?——I little thought
to have heard such language from you.——
Could you be so simple as to suppose that
Rosetta should ever be the wife of lord
Darnley?"—

I was distracted; and, as he attempted to
proceed, I started up, and, snatching a
knife

knife which lay upon the chimney-piece,
" This," I cried, " ſhall rid me of my
ſorrows."—

He ſprung to me, and ſeized the weapon
from my hand.

" No," continued I, falling back upon a
ſeat; " no, barbarian, thou ſhalt not baffle my
reſolution to deſtroy a life which thou haſt
rendered odious to me.——Monſter, thou
haſt robbed me of my honour, a bleſſing
infinitely preferable to that of exiſtence;
and wouldſt thou now prevent me from
putting a period to that exiſtence, from
putting a period to my ſhame and miſery?—
Cruel man!—Send me back to the place
which bears teſtimony to my innocence;—
reſtore me to that innocence which was my
only wealth;—reſtore me to my unhappy
parents—to whom—alas! I am now a diſ-
grace.——Permit me to breathe my laſt ſigh
upon

upon their bofom.——Ah ! my lord, have I merited this punifhment; or if I have, ought I to receive it from thee ?"—

And he advanced to me, holding out his hand.

" Villain, add not hypocrify to thy crimes—Appear, as thou art, my deftroyer, the deftroyer of a whole family.——And canft thou be fo barbarous as to refufe me death ?—The grave is the only afylum for me, and fhall I not be fuffered to plunge into it ?——Heaven furely will take pity on a wretch who has not another refource."—

Tears and fobs choked my utterance. I was overwhelmed in a ftupor of grief. His lordfhip retired, feemingly confounded, after having whifpered fome directions to the young woman who waited on me. This creature, affected with my fituation,

exerted

exerted every effort to confole me. She told me, that my lord feemed to be moved, and that he would certainly efpoufe me. But the veil was torn off; and it was no longer poffible to deceive me. The villany of Darnley had funk into my heart in all its horror; and at length the maid conducted, or rather dragged, me to my apartment.

There I gave myfelf up to a crowd of ideas, which vanifhed fucceffively. " It is eafy to die," thought I, " to throw off the burthen of a life, which I am no longer able to fupport.——But have I not fufficiently offended againft Religion and Virtue already?—Shall I add to my crimes?—To perifh!—to perifh, without once more beholding my dear parents!——Ah! let me pour my tears, my foul, into their bofom!—let their kifs be imprinted on my expiring lips."——

At

At length, after a tide of jarring emotions, having fixed upon a fcheme, I affumed an air of compofure; and my attendant, imagining that I was going to fall afleep, left me. Determined to execute my project immediately, I dreffed myfelf in my ruftic habit. " Alas!" thought I, wettting it with my tears, as I put it on; "this reminds me of my happy ftate of obfcurity—reminds me that I once was virtuous.——O moft affectionate of mothers, moft venerable of fathers, deign to receive me once more into your arms, to enjoy at leaft the confolation of expiring at your feet, of expiring with your laft bleffing."—

I left behind me all the poifoned prefents which Darnley had lavifhed upon me. Shocked at the thought of retaining aught that belonged to my bafe feducer, I carried with me no ornament but a ring of fmall value, which had been prefented to me by

one

one of my relations, and which I intended to difpofe of before I left London. With what fhame, what indignation, did I behold the fplendid robes, the diamonds, with which the traitor had adorned my difhonour! With my new drefs, I feemed, in fome meafure, to have recovered that innocence, the lofs of which I fhall, to eternity, deplore.

My apartment was on the firft ftory; and from one of the windows of it, by the help of a curtain, I effected my efcape. Previous to my departure from this hated abode, I wrote a letter to his lordfhip, which contained nearly, thefe expreffions; for forrow has rooted them in my memory.

" Unwilling to kill myfelf, becaufe I yet dread the vengeance of that Heaven, which I have already offended, and becaufe I wifh to breathe my laft figh upon the bofom of my parents, I have formed a refolution, the

only

only one which is proper for my fituation; that of detefting thee, of flying from thee for ever, as my mortal foe, as the deftroyer of the only blefling which an unhappy girl poffefled.

"Perfidious Darnley!—Thou haft torn me from the arms of my father and mother, haft fported with the moft facred oaths, haft robbed me of what is a thoufand times more valuable than life, my honour; and, in reward of my credulity, thou haft loaded me with infamy.——Barbarous man!—There was not a heart more fervently devoted to virtue than mine.—With what eyes will my parents, who have paffed a life of fixty years without reproach, behold a daughter, who, though fhe has not numbered feventeen, is already a difgrace to her family, and to the place in which fhe was born?—With fuch guilt upon me, my lord, I find life intolerable. From the bed of death, the

voice

voice of my forrow, my defpair, fhall reach to thee, fhall accufe, torment, thee. Then perhaps remorfe will find a paffage to thy foul, and thou wilt beftow a tear upon me when it is too late.——Remember, my lord, that all I afked was, the name of wife for one moment, that I might die with ho-nour.——Not a foul is there upon earth to protect me, to fupport me, to reprefent to thee my injured innocence.——I leave thee to the vengeance of God.——Tremble, there-fore; and reflect, that the weak, though they are oppreffed upon earth, have yet a powerful defender in heaven.

" P. S. Thou wilt find in my apartment all thy perfidious prefents.——I have re-fumed my former habit, the only one which becomes me.—Would I could, with that, have refumed my former innocence !——I carry with me naught but a heart broken by remorfe ; and I embrace with joy a ftate of

mifery,

mifery, for which I fhall have no caufe to blufh."

Having got into the ftreet, I walked forward in great hafte, ftill apprehenfive that I was not far enough from that fatal abode. Every joint of me trembled, and I was bewildered in darknefs. I heard a noife, and I doubled my fpeed. The noife followed me. " What, Mifs," cried a man, feizing me by the arm, " abroad at thefe hours!— Whither are you gadding?"

I difcovered that it was lord Darnley's chaplain.

" Ah! Mr. Hickman," I cried, " in the name of God, protect me,—force me not to return to that abominable houfe. Thou canft not perform an action more worthy of thy facred office.——I have bid a final adieu to lord Darnley; and it is my wifh to be

re-admitted

re-admitted into the bofom of virtue, into the bofom of my parents.——Thou haft the power to give me affiftance——deny it not, I conjure thee."——

The wretch, who did not live in Darnley-houfe, told me, that though his wife was from home, yet I fhould find a fecure afylum under his roof. He prefented his arm to me, and conducted me to his abode. I fat down; and, in a few words, I told him all my forrows.——Would you believe it, Sir?—— The villain, whofe pity and charitable compaffion I thought I had excited, taking advantage of my diftrefs, addreffed me in a ftyle widely different from the fpirit of his character. I faw my imprudence, but it was too late to repair it. The monfter offered violence. I threw myfelf at his feet, I remonftrated, I intreated, I wept, I fobbed.——" Alas! Sir," I exclaimed, "haft thou renounced the duties of religion, of

                    K                    nature,

nature, of humanity ? I confidered thee as a guardian angel, thy houfe as the temple of honour.——And wouldft thou abufe the confidence of a wretch, who, next to protection from heaven, implores protection from thee ?————

The unfeeling villain renewed his attempts; and I fprung to the window, fcreaming out, " Will no one come to the relief of an unhappy girl ?"—In a rage he threw a handkerchief over my mouth. A violent knocking was heard; and Hickman refufed to open the door. The knocking increafed; and inftantly a young gentleman in a military garb, having forced a paffage, rufhed forward with a drawn fword in his hand.

I threw myfelf at his feet,————

" Oh !"

" Oh !" exclaimed I, " whoever thou
art, fave me from the villany of the worft of
men."——

The ftranger eagerly raifed me up, and
feated me befide him. I then told him, without difguife, the accident which had expofed
me to the violence of Hickman. " Put
your truft in me," he cried ; " and let me
convince you, that though bred to arms, I
yet am not afhamed to be the champion of
virtue.——As for thee, wretch," turning to
Hickman, " thy meannefs protects thee.——
But for that thou hadft not at this moment
exifted.——Come, mifs, follow me."——

My deliverer was feemingly about five or fix
and twenty, and of an engaging form. Magnanimity was painted on his countenance. I
refigned myfelf to his generofity, with a refolution to put an end to my exiftence, if,
like Hickman, he fhould have the bafenefs



to

to betray my confidence; and I perfuaded myfelf that the Almighty, in confideration of my motive for it, would pardon me that laft offence.

Behold me then in the ftreets of London, at midnight, alone with a young officer, and, in fome meafure, at his difcretion. I had hardly ftrength to fupport myfelf. He perceived that my terror increafed at every ftep. —" Once more, mifs," faid he to me, " let me intreat you to banifh every fear, to rely upon my probity, and to believe, that, tho' young, I yet am not callous to the impreffions of virtue, or infenfible to the pleafure which refults from a difcharge of the duties of honour."

My diftrefs hardly permitted me to hear him. We reached Norfolk-ftreet; and he introduced me into a plain but elegant apartment.——" I have only two rooms," faid he.

he, " this, and one upon the fecond floor.—
Repofe yourfelf here for a few hours ; and
in the morning I will conduct you to
my mother, who lives a few miles from
town.  There we fhall be able to conceal
you from the bafe Darnley ; and from thence,
if you will give me leave, I will accompany
you to your parents."————

I looked up to my protector ; and I knew
not whether, after the cruel trial I had undergone, I ought to give faith to fuch generous proceedings.  We fat down to a cold
repaft : and he told me that his name was
Sir Edward Warboys ; that he was an only
fon ; that he belonged to the navy ; and that
chance had brought him under the windows
of Hickman's houfe, when, hearing my
cries, he flew to my affiftance.——

Tears were the only anfwer I could give
to him.

" You weep, mifs!" continued he.——
" Believe me, I feel your diftrefs.——You
are now, however, returning to the place
of your nativity, where you will forget your
bafe feducer, and become again the pleafure
and the comfort of your worthy parents."—

And he rofe, and took his leave of me.

My diftruft ftill continued ; and having
carefully fecured the door, I fat down, oppreffed with forrow, upon an elbow-chair,
determined not to go to bed, or to clofe my
eyes.

I have already told you, that if Sir Edward
fhould follow the example of Hickman, I
had refolved to deftroy myfelf.  I rofe ; and,
falling on my knees, I implored, from the
bottom of my foul, the protection of heaven.  I then refumed my feat with more
affurance ; for God read my heart, and faw
in it true repentance.———How often does

his

his providence manifeſt itſelf when we are in the midſt of dangers, and when even hope forſakes us!———In ſpite of every effort, ſleep, at length, ſurpriſed me ; and a dream yet heightened my diſtreſs.

I fancied that I was in a cavern, which was enlightened with one gloomy lamp, and that I was about to plunge into a grave, when an old man, whoſe grey locks veiled his face, preſented himſelf before me.

" This grave," exclaimed he, " is not deſtined for thee.—It is mine.—My; daughter has brought me to it."———

I diſcovered him to be my father, and advanced to embrace him.

" Away!" continued he, " or if thou comeſt near, cover me with that cloth."—

And

· And I found in my hand a fhroud. I fhrieked ; and with the rattling of earth thrown upon a coffin, I heard a voice from the grave pronounce thefe words, " Here it is that we expeĉt thee."——

I awaked in horror. The candle was out; and I heard Sir Edward's voice.

" Come, mifs," cried he, " open the door : it is time to fet out.————And have you not been in bed !———— That dif- truft," continued he, with a look of ten- dernefs, falls me.————Think you that all men are equally deteftable as Darnley and Hickman, that becaufe they are infen- fible, fenfibility does not exift ?"——

" Generous man," replied I, " this is an addition to the guilt of that unworthy lord and his chaplain.—They have taught me to form a judgment of all men by them.——I

fin_

fincerely beg your pardon for the miftake—.
Yes, Sir, I am convinced that you are truly
fenfible of the merit of a noble deed ; and
there is not perhaps one which is . more fo
than that of protecting an unhappy woman,
who wifhes to return to the paths of virtue."--

Tea was ordered in, and we fet off at
break of day.

Lady Warboys, in whom were ftill to be
difcovered the traces of beauty, poffeffed a
certain dignity, a certain charm, which fur-
vive the graces of figure ; and fhe received
me with an air of benevolence that expelled
from my bofom the timidity of misfortune.
Her fon recounted the ftory of my diftrefs ;
and I, without referve, confeffed my errors.
My ingenuity affected her ; and fhe conde-
fcended to embrace me, to receive my tears
into her bofom.

I paffed

I paſſed ſeveral days under the roof of this worthy family, which ſeemed to be the aſy-lum, the refuge, of the unhappy. Though deeply impreſſed with gratitude for the kind-neſſes which were heaped upon me by lady Warboys, and by Sir Edward, yet I longed, with unabated impatience, to behold again my parents. My protectreſs obſerved that I did ; and ſhe addreſſed me in words which I ſhall never forget.

" I ſhould be ſorry, Roſetta, to de-tain you here any longer.————Lord Darnley, I ſuppoſe, baffled in his inquiries, has now relinquiſhed his deteſtable project of preventing your return to your family.— Go then, my dear girl, and throw yourſelf into their arms.——Next to the ſoul which has defied the allurements of vice, is that ſoul which is devoted to penitence.——For-get not, that imprudence, which has been the ſource of your failings, has been the

ſource

source of misery to many of the youth of our sex ; and be assured, Rosetta,"—while she clasped me in her arms—" be assured, that virtue is no chimera, that it is an object of homage even to those who believe not in it.———Reflect, that honour is superior to every thing ; that neither wealth nor grandeur can redeem the loss of it ; and that, when lost, a repentance, sincere as yours seems to be, can alone wipe off the stain of it.———On Darnley's head lies all the guilt. He has been so base as to take advantage of your youth, of your weakness ; and heaven will avenge you.———May your error cease not to inspire you with a diffidence of yourself!———Be not ashamed to return to the labours of the field.———Consider, that they were the primitive, that they are still the most honourable, the most innocent, employments of man; that, though fatiguing, they are yet unattended with meanness. While our fathers laboured the

ground,

ground, they were honeſt, they were lovers of virtue.  Avarice drew them to cities; and when they relinquiſhed the plough, they relinquiſhed the duties of their being.  Their puniſhment has been ſevere,  for they are no longer capable of enjoying the pleaſures of nature.  It was not a labourer, my girl, who ſeduced you.————No:————it was a lord, one of the framers of · our laws, and whoſe duty it was to  have been a protector of them.————Bluſh not  to ſtand forth an example  to your  fellow-peaſants;  to tell them that your  fate  will  be  theirs,  if they  guard  not  againſt  the  ſnares  of ſeduction.————Your tears  have doubtleſs moved  the ſupreme being; and why ſhould they not find a paſſage to the hearts of men?————They  will  pardon  you—pardon!———— they will love you.————There  is  nothing ſo affecting as repentance when it is ſincere. ————Adieu, my dear Roſetta!————write to us; and be aſſured, that in me, and in

my

my fon, you have found friends who will never defert you."——

I funk in tears upon the ground, at the feet of her ladyfhip, who eagerly raifed me up, and again embraced me with all the warmth of an affectionate mother.

I prepared for my journey; but Sir Edward found means to put it off for fome days longer.——Often did I mark his eyes, wet with tears, riveted upon me;—often with a figh did he throw his trembling hand upon mine;—and often, in attempting to fpeak to me, he could only utter my name.

At length, after a number of delays and pretences, the hour of my departure arrived; and Sir Edward was the firft to haften it.—— My benefactrefs had complaifantly put a piece of money into my hand in return for the ring which I had refolved to fell before my departure from London.   I took my leave of her with forrow ; and though I entreated her fon not to accompany me as he propofed, he yet perfifted in his defign.

On the road, Sir Edward feemed to be engroffed by a gloomy melancholy.——He fighed, but feldom fpoke.   We were to feparate at a village about three miles diftant from mine.   As we advanced to it, his forrow encreafed ; and he perpetually enquired of me how far we had to go.   At length we alighted, and I thanked my protector, and wept.

" To heaven," faid I, " to heaven, which can alone requite the obligations I owe to thee, do I leave it to reward thee."—

" And muft we part !" replied he.

" We

" We muſt.———It is time for me to fly to my parents, to die at their feet."—

" Adieu !" ſaid we to each other———
" Adieu !"

He ſeized my hand ; and I felt it wet with tears.  He gazed upon me with a deep ſigh ; and with words upon his lips, he fell down in a ſwoon.

I ſcreamed ; and the people of the inn immediately flew to his relief.  On his re-covery, they left us ;  and I told him my diſtreſs at this accident.

" Roſetta," ſaid he, " let me beg of you to ſit down, to liſten to what I have to ſay."—

And he again took hold of my hand.

I wiſhed

- " I wifhed to have been filent, but I find that it is impoffible ; and I cannot bid an eternal farewell to you, without revealing to you my ftory."——

" Prompted by humanity alone, I rufhed to your affiftance.——Your fituation melted me.————I no fooner beheld you than I felt my bofom glow with a paffion pure though it was violent. Your misfortunes, your tears, your ingenuity, heightened your charms.————I could not withhold from you my refpect, my adoration.——To my love then, not to my generofity, afcribe the fervice I have done to you; and know, from this confeffion, that I do not merit, that I do not require, an acknowledgment for it. ———— My love for you ftill increafed. I was infenfible to every pleafure but that of feeing you, when, as a laft effort of integrity, which you perhaps obferved, I fuddenly, after a number of delays, urged your depar-

ture,

ture.——Hear my motive for it.——My mother, whom I tenderly love, has concluded for me a match with a diftant relation; and if I fhould difappoint her, fhe would be unhappy.——To her will, therefore, I fhall yield myfelf a facrifice.——I fhall marry the woman of her choice, though fortune has prefented to me the woman of my heart.—Yes, dear Rofetta, I would have endeavoured to repair the wrongs you fuftained from the bafe Darnley, would have rewarded injured virtue in you.——But no more of a love which I muft ftifle!——I expect not even an anfwer from you; and I leave you in the hope that you will at leaft lament for me."—

And with thefe words, he rofe haftily, flew to his chariot, and difappeared.

A conduct fo noble could not fail to heighten my gratitude.—But how great was my aftonifhment when I found in my pocket a diamond, which, to me, feemed to be of confiderable value ! I immediately dif-patched a letter to the generous Sir Edward, in which I intreated that he would continue his friendfhip for me, and that he would take back a prefent which would humble me in his eyes and in my own. I added, that if fentiments independent of love would fuffice, thefe I would chearfully beftow upon him without referve.————Alas ! Sir"————

And the adorable girl fighed.

" Alas ! Sir, I was then a ftranger to love.————I finifhed my letter, with an earneft requeft, that he would compleat the happinefs of his mother by efpoufing his relation, and with repeating, that a wretch like me, inftead of yielding to any tender attachment, ought to fpend her days in perpetual tears for her guilt. The clergyman

gyman of the place recommended to me a trufty meffenger; and I charged him to deliver the diamond and the letter to Sir Edward in perfon.

With what a crowd of emotions was I overwhelmed as I approached to my native village!——Shame, joy, grief, took at once poffeffion of my foul.———I enquired of a ftranger who paffed me about my parents; and I was informed——O God! and I—— I am the caufe of it———I was informed, that they had quitted their refidence, the fpot of their nativity, difconfolate for the lofs of me, and bewailing doubtlefs my life, more cruel to them than would have been my death.———My dear parents!"———I have never feen them more, Sir; have never been able to learn to what place they had retired.——Alas! devoted as they were to religion and to virtue, forrow muft, ere now, have brought them to the grave.——

I re-

I returned upon my footſteps, looking back every moment upon my dear village. ——Sometimes I thought that I eſpied our thatched cottage; and the image of it tore my heart.——Oh! cruel, cruel Darnley!———

At length I arrived at the ſpot in which you firſt ſaw me, where I am employed in the meaneſt offices.—Alas! can I ever expiate the errors of my paſt life?—Yet in the midſt of my misfortunes, I have one comfort. At the age of eighteen, inſtead of waiting to be torn from vice, I have had the reſolution to tear myſelf from it. I ſhall live—I ſhall die in tears. The ſincerity, the fervour, of my repentance will perhaps render me leſs criminal in the eye of my offended Maker.——Could I but have the comfort of embracing the dear authors of my being, of watering with my tears their venerable wrinkles, of being the prop of

their

their old age !——But have I not been the cause of their death ?—I have. They were unable to survive my dishonour.——— Mine !—they have themselves been tainted by it. Yes, I have dug their grave ;— have deprived them of life, in return for having given it to me, in return for the favours they heaped upon me. My dream, I doubt not, is realized :—from their daughter——— a daughter whom they loved with so much tenderness, they have received their mortal stab.—

Alas ! Sir, from this faithful narrative, determine my duty and your own. Though I cannot accept of your hand, yet I confess, that I love you. It is an addition to my misfortunes.——Be my friend, then, my protector ; honour me, with your advice ; grieve for my fate ; but renounce a project which could not fail to be injurious to us both.——Leave me to mourn the loss of my honour ; to mourn that I can

never

never be yours. —— Farewell, Sir! You cannot have any thing to anfwer.—Come, Emily, let us return."——

It is impoffible, Charles, to defcribe to thee the different hurricanes that arofe in my breaft. I beheld Rofetta the victim of feduction and villany, at a period of life when every furrounding object dazzles ;—beheld her, reftored to virtue, with her charms in full bloom.——A female of eighteen fpurning from her every pleafure, embracing the moft abject condition, the moft horrid mifery, and ready to die with remorfe !———What a picture, my friend ! and how deeply is it engraved on my heart !

Thus I wrote to the miftrefs of my heart.

" Rofetta, I have weighed every obftacle, and I am determined. Your penitence is fincere :—you are enamoured Virtue,

and

and you confefs your love for me.——They
who, having loft their honour, retain a
fenfe of the value of it, have recovered it.—
Even my reafon pleads for you;—pleads,
that I fhould make you my wife, and tells
fne, that I fhall never have another."

Hear her anfwer.

" Yes, Sir, I do love you; and in return
for my fenfibility, you tear me from the
only happinefs it was left me to enjoy.—
Pure friendfhip alone could have dried up
my tears;—and you deny me even that confolation.  I fhall inftantly fly from this retreat, never to fee you more.—Adieu, then,
for ever!——Alas! Sir, ought I to accept
of your hand?—I, who deferve not to be a
wife to the meaneft of men?——No: preferve your honour in its purity, .and let my
.difgrace be my own.  Away with the
thought!——They who can truly repent,

can

can die.——In this world we ſhall not be united.—Take, then, the all which it is in my power to grant to you, my tears, my eſteem, my love.——Would I had aught elſe in my power!———Be aſſured, Sir, that affection alone prompts me to this ſtep.——It may coſt me my life.—My life! of what avail is that?—Yet, it is the only ſacrifice I can make to you."

I flew to the farm-houſe, and found the family in tears. Roſetta had diſappeared, after having left them a few trifling preſents. The worthy people expatiated on her excel_lent qualities, on the loſs they had ſuſtained. Twenty times did they repeat, that an angel could not poſſeſs more ingenuity, more benevolence.—Father, mother, child_ren, all regretted my dear Roſetta. I made them recount the moſt minute cir_cumſtance that related to her. She had wept bitterly before her departure;—wept,

and

and repeatedly pronounced my name.——
Conceive my diftraction.——My foul darted
into every path through which Rofetta
might have paffed.  I fearched every village
in the neighbourhood, made every poffible
enquiry, but in vain.—It is almoft needlefs
to add, that Villars was my confident.

In a folitary excurfion, one evening, on
horfeback, I wandered I knew not whither.
Ready to fink with fatigue, I alighted at
the entrance of a wood.  At a little diftance,
I efpied a miferable hut, from whence proceeded a glimmering light.  Impelled by
what motive I know not, I advanced toward
it, and heard a voice utter, as if with difficulty, " Oh! my father, mother, my
dear, dear parents, do I ftill force tears from
you?—I have offended you, have brought
difhonour upon your old age;—and it is
juft that I fhould die.——Alas! It was my
wifh to have been the comfort and the prop
of it.——Can you pardon me?"

" Pardon

" Pardon thee! Yes, dear child.—Embrace us, and put thy truft in Heaven, which will reftore thee to health, and fuffer us to die.———Our grave is under out feet, ready to receive us."—

" Alas! it is in vain to think of recalling me to life.—I die with remorfe—die with—but you will hereafter learn the other caufe of my death.———I have only one favour to afk."—

" Dear Rofetta!"———

" Soon as my eyes are clofed, fee that this letter is delivered, agreeably to the direction.—It is for Sir Henry Lenox, and he is to be found at Villars-Abbey."—

I rufhed into the cottage.———A woman, expiring upon the bed of Poverty, with a letter in her hand; an aged man in

tears,

tears, who veiled her face with his filver locks; another woman, alfo aged, alfo in tears, who clafped one of her hands in her's, prefented themfelves before me. I fprung forward, and fnatched the letter.—Read the contents of it.

" To you, O worthy man, fuperior to the reft of your fex, I addrefs my laft fighs. I may now pour out my foul to you, fince, ere this letter fhall reach you, I fhall be no more.——Know then, dear Sir Henry, that I die for you, that I fhunned you becaufe it was my duty, becaufe I could not, with your heart, enjoy your name. Gratitude would have induced me to reject the hand of Sir Edward Warboys, if he had been at liberty to make an offer of it to me.—— Think then what love owes to you.—— How fenfible have you made me of the fatal confequences which attend the lofs of virtue!—I refpected your honour; and I

feel

feel myself unable to survive my sorrow
that I am no longer worthy to enjoy that
society, in which my soul seemed to resume
its strength, its purity, its innocence. In
dying, I give you a proof of the sincerity of
my affection.——As my friend, my only
friend, may I presume to beg, that you
will bestow a small portion of your bounty
upon my poor parents?——Alas! I am
the cause of all their misery. Grief for—
shall I call it my fault?—No: grief for my
guilt hath rendered them incapable of pre-
serving the trifle of wealth which they pof-
sessed. They blushed for their unhappy
daughter—they, who never had aught to
reproach themselves with, but that they had
given birth to me. They had retired to a
wretched cottage;—there I found them,
there I now expire. They have deigned to
open their arms to me; and I have once
more enjoyed the happiness of pressing to
my heart the dear authors of my being.——

Let

Let them remind you of the unhappy Rofetta; and be affured, that my foul will feel, and be grateful for, every favour they fhall owe to you.——Adieu for ever, dear Sir Henry. I embrace death as a bleffing, fince I have loft what alone could render me refpectable in the eyes of the only man I ever truly loved."

I fcreamed out, " Ah, my dear Rofetta!"—

The good people were confounded; and Rofetta, having opened her eyes, funk into my arms in a fwoon. I cannot finifh the fcene, my friend :—thy feeling heart will be full of it.

" Yes, my dear Rofetta," continued I, with all the tranfport of love; " yes, you fhall be my wife:—our hearts are already united. In rewarding you, I fhall reward Virtue itfelf. To err, is the lot of huma-

nity;

nity; to rife fuperior to our failings by a fincere repentance, is to merit that efteem which is due to the moft unfullied virtue."—

" And you," faid I to the venerable couple, who were at my feet, " you fhall be my father and mother; I fhall be your fon, your fecond child.——Rofetta and I will have no other conteft, but which fhall love you, cherifh you, the moft."—

Such then is my fituation, Charles.— The fight of me has reftored Rofetta to life, though fhe ftill perfifts that fhe cannot be mine. I have told her, however, that my life depends upon her compliance. We are now at Villars-Abbey, where preparations are making for the wedding. My Rofetta is fprung from a race of hufband-men, who have been models of virtue in the village in which they lived. It is my inten-tion to pafs my days in the country.—Long

have

have I lived for others, now let me live for myfelf, liften to the dictates of reafon, of my heart, and obey them. The ftudy of Nature, and of my own being, fhall fupply the place of converfations, in which fervile complaifance and dark perfidy affume the name of a focial difpofition, and of polite-nefs. My wife will feel the importance of her duty; and I am convinced, that, if fhe becomes a mother, fhe will love, and will know how to bring up, her child;——am convinced, that nothing can fhake her grati-tude, her attachment, to me.——There are moments, I confefs, in which I refume my chains, in which I fubmit to the fentiments of the vulgar, in which I hear, even at this diftance, the buzz of St. James's.——But when I return into myfelf, when I give ear to truth, can I entertain a doubt that Ro-fetta is not a real penitent? Why, then, fhould fhe not be rewarded?——Is not real penitence the moft effectual atonement?

and

and are not juſtice and benevolence the greateſt of pleaſures?—Say, Charles, what muſt I do?——

## FROM CHARLES NEWBURGH, ESQ: TO SIR HENRY LENOX, IN ANSWER.

Marry Roſetta, my friend;—do what a being ſuperior to man would do in your place.——Reſtore to that unhappy girl her honour, by ſhielding it with your own, Since you are convinced, that ſhe loves you, that ſhe ſincerely grieves for her errors, that ſhe attempts not to deceive you, reward her for her reſolution in flying from vice, at an age in which ſhe might have given charms to it.——Roſetta is truly virtuous. Her ſoul is ſtill untainted; and it is on the villain alone who betrayed her innocence, that the contempt of the world ought to fall. You talk of burying yourſelf in the country with your wife and new relations.—

Beware

Beware of that. Have you done a bad action?
——No : you have overcome prejudice,
and trampled it under foot.——Come, then,
to London : insult it there, and display
your elevated foul in all its lustre. Come,
and teach men, that, by forsaking their
hacknied paths of ignorance, and of folly, you
rise superior to them. Feel, Henry, in its
utmost extent, the service you do to humanity.- ——You render virtue its own reward,
by re-exalting to her native greatness a
fellow-creature, degraded in her own eyes,
because she was degraded in those of the vulgar, who know not the true value of any
thing. You do more, my friend. By this
glorious example you snatch from the con-
tagion of vice a multitude of charming creatures, who will see that virtue has, even on
earth, its comforts and its recompence, and
who will hope to find hearts generous as your
own. Enjoy your happiness, Henry. I long
to clasp you in my arms.——And those wor-

thy people!————Are you thoroughly sen-
fible of the joy you have given to them?
———— You have reftored to them their
daughter, their honour, have fcattered flowers upon the laft ftage of their earthly journey. Woe to that foul which feels not, in
its utmoft latitude, the magnanimity of your
conduct, which partakes not of your happinefs. You are, in my efteem, a hero infinitely more deferving of applaufe than the
moft diftinguifhed warrior. He acts not
but on the principles of falfe glory. If
the town fhould be fo weak as to with-
hold from you that applaufe, turn to your
heart, my friend, and that will tell you,
you have done a glorious deed. Let that
teftimony fatisfy you; and with it accept of mine, the teftimony of an affectionate friend. Let me repeat it, Henry,
what would a being more than human do in
your place? What you have done, and what
I fhall ever admire. From his approbation
of your choice, I fhall entertain a much
more

more high opinion of Lord Villars than I did. I am impatient for your arrival. Make hafte then, my friend, for this wretched world ftands in need of examples. You fhall be the true philofopher. I am tired of reading treatifes of morality, and feeing fo little of it practifed.————How many hufbands will you confound, who are yoked with women, who profane the very name of wife! Thefe are the objects who deferve contempt. Would the ridiculous chatter of our lordlings give you any uneafinefs?—Leave them to their own worthy mates, and Rofetta will be amply revenged. I am on the rack till I fee her.————Adieu, courageous fage. I hardly know what I write, fo much am I charmed with the manlinefs of your proceeding. Our little coterie falute you. Already have we emptied an hundred bumpers to the health of lady Lenox.————

P. S.

P. S.  The town rings with the news of your marriage.  I obſerved, that at firſt it occaſioned much ſurpriſe.  People of merit have not the reſolution to judge for themſelves.  They attempt it ; but it is by ſlow degrees that the light of reaſon appears.  Your preſence will determine them.  Lord Ruſport inſiſts, that, for one Roſetta, he would give a thouſand ſuch beings as the world call " honeſt women."  Our witlings, I doubt not, will ſoon talk themſelves down ; and to what advantage, my friend, will you appear, when viewed through the medium of truth !


END of the FIRST VOLUME.

# THE

# TEARS of SENSIBILITY,

# NOVELS:

### NAMELY,

1. THE CRUEL FATHER.
2. ROSETTA; OR, THE FAIR PENITENT RE-WARDED.
3. THE RIVAL FRIENDS.
4. SIDNEY AND SILLI; OR, THE MAN OF BE-NEVOLENCE AND THE MAN OF GRATITUDE.

Tranſlated from the French of

## M. D' ARNAUD,

## BY JOHN MURDOCH.

## VOL. II.

## LONDON:

Printed for EDWARD and CHARLES DILLY, in the Poultry.

MDCCLXXIII.

# THE

# RIVAL FRIENDS.

THE Chevalier de Selicourt, a youth of an engaging appearance, and with noble blood in his veins, was sent by his father to Paris, as the most proper place to receive an education which might fit him for the profession of arms.

Eager to acquire wisdom, at an age when people seem to value themselves upon a ne-



glect

glect of it, the chevalier, even in the midst of dissipation, found time for reflection ; and experience already told him, how wide the difference is between true love and a transient engagement, the almost inevitable consequences of which are, languor and disgust. His heart was susceptible of one passion only. A tender, and at the same time a solid attachment therefore was the sole object of his wishes ; and by a fortunate event they were at length gratified.

The charms of the Baroness Darmilli, and of the Marchioness de Menneville, had for some time attracted an equal degree of admiration. The baroness had been left a widow after a marriage of a few months. Her figure was regular to admiration, her shape at once elegant and majestic, and her soul so ductile as to adapt itself to every different *ton*. But so predominant was her passion for government and tyranny—a passion, which, even in a sex formed to subdue us, offends

our

our pride, and difgufts us—that though all acknowledged the power of her beauty, yet all were unwilling to yield to it. She was furrounded with admirers; and the poffeffion of an ample fortune gave no fmall luftre to her attractions. Notwithftanding her haughtinefs, fhe was not deftitute of fenfibility. To form a choice, however, that might flatter her vanity, was her vice; and, fuch was her difpofition, there was not any danger that felf would be facrificed to love.

Nature feemed to have formed the marchionefs as a contraft to Madame Darmilli. Two large black eyes, fraught with an affecting languor, rendered the utterance of her fentiments in fome meafure unneceffary. She appeared as if afraid to be thought handfome by the world, and as if defirous to conceal from herfelf that fhe really was fo. Every day gave new charms to her. Her converfation was rather affecting than brilliant; and hardly a word efcaped from her

which

which did not convey a sentiment. Her parents, paying less attention to inclination than to interest, agreeably to the general mode, had sacrificed her to a husband from whom she experienced every mortification which old age and jealousy can inflict; a husband, who, confiding more in his own vigilance than in the virtue, the blameless conduct, of his wife, had his dishonour, which he dreaded yet less than the ridicule that would attend it, perpetually before him.

Different as they were in feature and in character, Madame Darmilli and Madame de Menneville were inseparable friends; and it was at a ball that they became acquainted with the Chevalier de Selicourt.

Though those passions that are conceived at first sight, which not unoften abide by us through life, are treated as chimerical, yet

thus

thus were Selicourt and the Marchionefs at once captivated with each other. The Chevalier became deeply enamoured. From the moment that he beheld Madame de Menneville, his eyes were riveted to her. A fenfation, hitherto unknown to him, engroffed his foul. He fighed, he felt a timidity upon him, he was afraid to fpeak. His wit loft its vivacity, he became abforbed in thought; and at length, aftonifhed at the diforder with which he was agitated, and convinced that his heart was about to refign itfelf for ever to all the violence of love, he left the company.

The marchionefs was equally at a lofs to account for the emotion which fhe had felt at the fight of the chevalier. Though in examining herfelf fhe was perhaps lefs fincere, yet Virtue whifpered to her a few reproaches, which fhe would have wifhed to be unfounded. That fhe had thought Seli-

court

court amiable, however, fhe could not conceal from herfelf. She endeavoured to banifh an idea which became every moment
more alluring ; and fhe promifed to herfelf
that fhe would never more behold the object of it. Faintly, however, was pronounced her every vow to maintain, even in
thought, her duty inviolate. Her heart
was perpetually in arms to combat this fyf-
tem of indifference.———How dreadful is
the conflict when reafon and inclination are
at variance!—— How feeble, how impo-
tent, is the moft approved. virtue when it is
oppofed by paffion !

Selicourt, on the other hand, abandoned
himfelf, without referve, to all the enthufiafm of his infant love. A thoufand times
did he fwear that, to his laft breath, he
would adore Madame de Menneville.

" But

" For ever," faid he, " fhall fhe reign the emprefs of my heart. Henceforth, my only care fhall be, to convince her that I love her with a tendernefs which death alone can terminate. One look from her will render me the happieft of men.——But if fhe fhould not love me—if fhe fhould love another.——What do I fay ?—I have not a wifh but to love her. If I am not permitted to fpeak to her of my paffion, I fhall at leaft enjoy the pleafure of thinking of it. That alone fhall engrofs my attention, fhall conftitute my happinefs."—

The baronefs was impatient to fee again Madame de Menneville ; and no fooner did they meet than the former began a converfation about Selicourt. The marchionefs, though fhe perceived that the encomiums of her friend upon their new acquaintance were too warm to be dictated by mere politenefs, had yet fo far the command of herfelf as to

conceal

conceal her uneafinefs ; and fhe took an early opportunity to withdraw.

"Is the baronefs then enamoured with Selicourt?" thought fhe as fhe returned home.—"Ah! wretch that I am, can I doubt it?——Yes, Selicourt is beloved by my friend!—Can I call her my friend who plunges into my heart a dagger?——Alas! my fituation is defperate. Whither does paffion hurry me?—Shall I admit thoughts which virtue rejects?——Shall I forget the ties, the facred ties, by which I am bound?——No: henceforth I will not think of, fee, the chevalier.——Is it in my power not to think of him?——Alas! can I have become already fo weak, fo guilty?——Yes, Selicourt I will never behold again.—— I will do more. If the baronefs loves him—*if* fhe loves him!—Too well am I convinced that fhe *does*.——Be it fo. Far from oppo- fing her inclination, I will arm her againft

my-

myself. She shall marry Selicourt.—How happy is she !——With her fortune she has it in her power to bestow her heart upon an object, who — why is Monsieur de Menneville not so amiable ?"—

Violent as her passion was, the marchioness retained so far the command of herself, as to avoid the company of Selicourt, while the baroness seized every opportunity to enjoy it. She even affected not to mention him. Madame Darmilli appeared, one day, absorbed in thought; and she tenderly enquired into the cause of it.

" You are my friend," answered she, after a look of eagerness, and a silence of a few moments"—" let me therefore beg your advice on one of the most important actions of my life."—

The

The marchionefs fhuddered.

" You have feen the chevalier de Sch-
court——feen him, and undoubtedly confeffed his charms.—For my own part, I—
I cannot help declaring him equally deferving of efteem as of love.—You do not
fpeak !"—

She coloured, and her confufion increafed.

" I entirely agree with you," replied
Madame de Menneville.—" His figure, I
am convinced, belies not his virtues."—

" A thought has ftruck me," continued
the baronefs, " and I hope, my dear, that
you will approve of it.——To be happy,
the heart, you know, muft be engaged ;
and as the moft fpotlefs virtue and an exquifite fenfibility are often infeparable, the
point is, to reconcile our inclination with

our

our duty. An agreeable hufband is preferable to a lover. With the former, inftead of blufhing at our happinefs, we are
proud of his love. I am almoft tempted,
therefore, to enter again into a ftate which
I formerly confidered as an intolerable bon-
dage, but would now prefer to liberty
itfelf.——Speak then, my dear marchionefs.
I am inclined to give my hand to Selicourt :—
your anfwer fhall determine me."—

What a ftroke was this to Madame de
Menneville!—To what a conflict was fhe
expofed!—Her doubts were now difpelled.
She beheld Madame Darmilli enamoured of
Selicourt—-beheld a rival in her friend.
She was at once afraid to betray a fhadow
of diffimulation to the Baronefs, and to
open her heart to her. Yet what could fhe
hope from a paffion which, as it could not
be gratified with honour, it was neceffary
to ftifle in its infancy: Even at the price of
the

the Chevalier's love, fhe would have been fatisfied, provided that he would continue difengaged from, and indifferent to, the reft of her fex. But every thing confpired againft her; and vain were all her efforts to fupprefs, or even to conceal, the different emotions which racked her foul.

" Heavens! my dear Marchionefs," cried Madame Darmilli, " you grow pale!"—

Madame de Menneville that inftant fell down in a fwoon. She was conveyed home, where, on opening her eyes, fhe perceived the following billet, written in an unknown hand.

" Let me intreat, madam, that if the firft expreffions of this letter fhould difpleafe you, you will not throw it afide, but perufe it to the end.

" I love

" I love you, madam —— reflect that I
have begged to be heard —— love you with
a tendernefs, a purity, that are inexpref-
fible. I know that your attachment to
virtue and to your duty is immoveable
—— know that I am unworthy of your
fmalleft notice; yet am I unable to conceal from you a paffion which every thing
confpires to oppofe. Permit me, however,
to enjoy the happinefs of thus declaring to
you that nothing can ever tear you from my
heart, that to my laft breath I fhall not
ceafe to adore you, without a return, without hope, without even the confolation of
hearing you fay that you pity me. Can
there be a more difinterefted homage ? Shall
I offend by feeling with rapture the power
of your charms and of your virtues, by dwel-
ling upon them in fecret, by repeating to
myfelf an hundred times, what I have determined never to repeat aloud, that you are
the moft adorable of women, I the moft affec-

tionate

tionate of lovers !—Affectionate of lovers !—
The expreſſion has eſcaped me, and I will not
eraſe it. Yes, I *am* the moſt affectionate, the
moſt unhappy, of lovers. If my preſence ſhall
offend you, I will even avoid every place
where there may be a poſſibility that we
ſhall meet.——What have I ſaid ?—Would
you deny me the happineſs of beholding you,
of enjoying from thoſe eyes, to which my
heart is unalterably riveted, a ſingle glance ?
—May it not ſuffice that I have impoſed upon myſelf an eternal ſilence ?—Would you
exact of me a greater ſacrifice ?———-Alas !
not to ſpeak to you of his love, and to die,
is all that is in the power of

The CHEVALIER de SELICOURT."


The feelings of Madame de Menneville
upon the peruſal of this epiſtle, are not to be
conceived. She found that the baroneſs was

not

not beloved, and that fhe had herfelf captivated a man whom fhe already adored. From her oppofition to it her paffion had gained ftrength, and at the fame time fhe was unwilling that it fhould triumph over her duty as a wife, and her generofity as a friend. "The fortune of Selicourt," thought fhe, "is flender; fhould he efpoufe my dear Madame Dar-milli, he would revel in opulence.—How happy fhall I be in fulfilling my duty, in facrificing my own happinefs to that of my friend, to that of the man who loves me, in foaring above the frailties of humanity!"—

Within a few days after the above circumftance, the chevalier received the following anonymous epiftle:

"You will doubtlefs be furprifed at the ftep I now take. Convinced that it is contrary to all the laws impofed upon my fex,

I am

I am myself aftonifhed at it, am myfelf the firft to pronounce my error. Yet am I unable, chevalier, to refift a paffion, to the nature of which, formed as you are to infpire it, you cannot be a ftranger.——Shall I call it friendfhip?—Alas! friendfhip excites not the emotions I feel. Spare me the confufion of making an acknowledgment which I expect from you with impatience. My happinefs depends upon your anfwer; and you may be yourfelf the meffenger of it. It is needlefs to tell you who I am: you muft have diftinguifhed me. Remember, however, if my franknefs is culpable, I flatter myfelf that, by you at leaft, I fhall not be judged with feverity."

" Judged with feverity!" echoed Selicourt, as he concluded the letter——" Ah! divine Menneville, with my life would I reward thee for this excefs of condefcenfion.——

Shall

Shall I impute to thee as a crime thy return to a paffion which is not more tender than it is refpectful ?——No :——I fly to adore thee."——

And in an inftant was the name of the chevalier de Selicourt announced to the marchionefs.  She happened to be alone.

" Your pity then, Madam," cried he, throwing himfelf upon his knees," has triumphed over your indifference.  My happinefs is too great to admit a doubt of it.— Let me die with love and joy at your feet ;—die repeating your name, repeating that I love you, that I adore you, that I have not a wifh to exift but for you.——Whither do you fly, Madam ? Would you leave me ! Has this declaration given offence to you ? Do you repent that you have rendered me the moft happy of men, who, till you pronounced my doom, was the moft wretched.

Deign then to raife upon me thofe eyes which add fuch luftre to your charms ——— deign"——

The marchionefs was fufpended between love, civility, and wonder; and thefe impreffions increafed at every word of the chevalier. She could not conceive to what it was owing that he addreffed her in fuch terms; and notwithftanding her virtue, fhe could not help enjoying a kind of pleafure in beholding at her feet the man of her heart.

"I am at a lofs, Sir," interrupted fhe, endeavouring to conceal her confufion, and raifing him from the ground;" "I am at a lofs, Sir, to comprehend what has given rife to this difcourfe, and vexed that curiofity fhould have prevailed upon me to liften to it.—You talk to me of your love, of a happinefs which it is far from being in my

power

power to confer upon you.——For heaven's
fake explain yourfelf."——

" It is I, Madam," refumed the chevalier
with warmth, " it is I who ought to beg
an explanation. Are you then unwilling to
alleviate the mifery of a man whofe tendernefs for you will carry him to the grave ?
You are. Too well do I perceive that you love
me not, that by this letter you meant to infult a paffion which I feel myfelf unable to
fubdue."—

And he put the fatal paper into her hand.
She read it, and the chevalier thus continued :

" To what do you advife me ?—Forget you
I cannot.—A thoufand deaths would I fuffer
in return for that inftance of generous condefcenfion, which you impute to yourfelf as
an indifcretion.——Take then a life which

I can

I can no longer enjoy than while I am permitted to adore you."—

. " Be seated, Sir," replied the marchioness, with a tone of resolution which gave the lie to her heart ;—" be seated, and hear what I have to say.——I desired that you would unfold the mystery of your behaviour, and I find that the task lies upon myself.— Allow me, Sir, in the first place, to ask you a few questions.—You have presumed to talk to me of love — love, which is too often the mere garb of perfidy — to write a letter to me full of it, · and yet you say, that you esteem, that you respect me !—— Know you not my situation, Sir ;—know you not that I ought to banish every idea that is in any degree inconsistent with the duty of a wife—of the wife of Monsieur de Menneville ?"—

" Too

" Too well, alas !" interrupted the chevalier with agitation, " do I know that I have a rival, and that that rival is a hufband. —But, Madam, I have already told you, and I now repeat it, that I am capable of loving, of adoring you, without a return, without hope. Nay, though you even hated me, you fhould engrofs my every wifh, fhould engrofs my foul, fhould be the unvaried object of a flame which death alone can extinguifh. Fear not my indifcretion. Sooner will I perifh than fuffer to efcape from me one word, one look, which may give offence to you.—Can a love like this be incompatible with refpect ?——Ah ! Madam, what heart is there fufceptible of a tendernefs like mine."—

Thefe words of the chevalier were uttered——might the expreffion be indulged—— with the tongue of perfuafion ; and the addition of a few tears rendered them not a

li tle

little formidable to the repofe and to the virtue of Madame de Menneville.——How anxious was fhe to triumph over them !—how fearful left her confufion fhould betray her !

" And to whom then, Madam," continued Selicourt, " am I indebted for this letter ?"—

" Not to me," replied Madame de Menneville with a figh.—It comes, Sir, from a lady who—who loves you, who has it in her power to beftow upon you her hand, and with it a fplendid fortune.——How great will be her happinefs !——You do not afk her name !"

" Yourfelf excepted, Madam, there is not upon earth a woman who can intereft my heart.——You talk to me of riches :——

riches !

riches! what are they when compared to love?"—

" You will find both, Sir, in your unknown correfpondent," replied the marchionefs, after a look full of tendernefs at the chevalier. " The lady has charms which ought to banifh from her all dread of a refufal; and I may, without a breach of difcretion, inform you that my friend, the Baronefs Darmilli, is fhe."—

" The Baronefs Darmilli, Madam!—— She is indeed poffeffed of every charm to captivate or to pleafe.——But"—added he in an affecting tone——" fhe is not Madame de Menneville!"——

" Her happinefs," refumed the marchionefs, " will be mine. Follow my advice, Sir, by paying your addreffes to her — but reveal not what I have told you.——Adieu.

A

A longer interview would—pray, Sir, allow me to be gone."—

And fhe inftantly withdrew into another
apartment. .

The chevalier was amazed at the abrupt-
nefs of her departure; and no fooner had he
left the houfe than the marchionefs gave
ftrict orders to deny all future admittance to
him. She fhut herfelf up in her clofet, and
abandoned herfelf to all the horror of her fituation.

" Well," thought fhe, " have I now
fatisfied this tyrant virtue?——At a time
when my réfolution had almoft forfaken me,
have I not facrificed every thing to my duty?
——I have. But ah! how dreadful was the
conflict when I beheld, at my feet, the man
I doat on; when I heard him declare his
love for me——his love, which cannot be
equalled but by my own!—Yet have I rejected

jected his tendernefs, and attempted to ftifle my own—have I told him that he is beloved by another, and fought to render that other happy.——Can friendfhip——friendfhip to which I am a victim—exact more of me ?—A victim to friendfhip !——Do I then forget that I have barely done what honour demands, that I am bound by ties which I am ⋅ compelled to revere ?—Whither would my guilty paffion hurry me ?——Am I not the wife of Monfieur de Menneville ?——Am I not fubject to him ?—Is not my chain—my chain indiffoluble ?"—

She continued for fome minutes abforbed in thought.

" Come," exclaimed fhe, ftarting up, " the chevalier fhall marry Madame Darmilli, and—and I will never fee him more."

Virtue

Virtue had not fled fo far from the breaft of the marchionefs as to render her infenfible of her weaknefs, or fearlefs of the confe-quences of it. She engaged her hufband to carry her, for a few months, into the country; and fhe actually waited upon the baronefs in order to take her leave of her.

Selicourt, in the mean while, had waited upon Madame Darmilli. In vain did he ex-ert his wit to enliven the converfation, while the baronefs, anxious to know what effect her billet had produced, perpetually led him to her favourite topic, perpetually extolled the fweets of a happy marriage, and painted, in every flattering colour, the plea-fures which wait on riches. Encomiums upon the beauty of the lady were the only anfwers of the chevalier;———encomiums, which, though they had in them more of gallantry than of love, were yet fo flattering to the vanity of Madame Darmilli, that fhe

took

took for declarations in form what were in reality mere fallies of wit, mere effufions of cold politenefs.

The baronefs was now convinced that fhe had made a conqueft——convinced that fhe had not fufficiently intimated her fentiments, and that the chevalier would have been more explicit if fhe had been lefs referved. Thus were affairs circumftanced when the marchionefs waited upon her with the news of her intended retreat into the country.

" The country, my dear !" exclaimed Madame Darmilli — " the country, when all the world flock to town'!——What can have given rife to this ftrange refolution ?"—

" I have my reafons for it.—I am tired of the town :—to you, my dear baronefs, it may have charms."—

" It

It has indeed at prefent, when I feem to be on the very brink of happinefs."—

" Happinefs !" interrupted Madame de Menneville, who trembled at every word fhe heard.

" Happinefs, my dear, with a man deferving of my hand.—I have feen Selicourt ; and to me he feems poffeffed of every quality to pleafe."—

" Then he loves you !"—

" He had no occafion to tell me that he does :—love eafily difcovers itfelf.—Let me then intreat, my dear friend, that you will ftay to witnefs our approaching union."—

" What ! you are going to marry him !"

And

.And that inftant the Marquis de Menneville was announced.


" Well, Madam," faid he to the marchionefs, " have you taken your leave of
the baronefs ?"—


In vain did fhe attempt to conceal her diforder.


" I have not, Sir.   The feafon is too far
advanced :—we will poftpone our journey."


" Why yefterday you was impatient to
fet out !"—


" Yefterday !—what we long for one day,
Sir, we often deteft the next.——Pray conduct me home."—


Monfieur de Menneville and Madame de
Darmilli looked at each other aftonifhed.
On her return, the marchionefs complained

of

of a violent head-ache, and begged to be left alone. Then did she feel to what a height her disorder had increased—feel, that love had assumed the entire possession of her soul.

" Never more," cried she, " shall I en-, joy tranquillity.——I am in love——dreadful idea !—in love with a man, who, at the time that he lavishes his adoration upon me, would sacrifice me to another—would—— No : he shall not marry the baroness.——I will discover every thing to her—will convince her of his perfidy.——Alas ! shall I be justified in doing this ? No : it was myself who urged the chevalier to reward the love of my friend.—My friend ! no longer is she entitled to that name.——She is my enemy, my barbarous, hateful enemy.——Ah ! wretch that I am, how dreadful are the effects of love ! I have lost my reason ; I abhor myself——abhor every thing but Selicourt.——O heaven ! let death be my

punish-

punishment — death, which can alone eradicate from my bosom a passion that is fraught with sorrow and with guilt, which can alone restore to me my tranquillity, my innocence."

A gloomy melancholy began already to prey upon the health of the marchioness.— Often did her husband surprise her in tears, often endeavour, but in vain, to penetrate the cause of them. She had given orders to deny all access to Selicourt, and she was every moment tempted to countermand them; she blamed herself for not having withdrawn into the country; and if she had done this, she would have returned to Paris the very same day.

Notwithstanding every obstacle, Selicourt found means to write to her. Twenty times did she peruse his letters, and accuse him, then condemn herself, and justify him. At

length

length she determined to send back to him those dangerous papers, which only served to feed in her a passion, which was without hope, and a despair, which was without cure. With his letters she sent to him the following billet :


" You persist then, Sir, in attempting to see me, in writing to me.  Instead of continuing to torment a heart which cannot, must not, be yours,  content yourself with the love of Madame Darmilli,  and make haste to con-firm to her a tendernefs of which she is al-ready convinced beyond a doubt.  From your implicit obedience to my past precepts, I doubt not your compliance now.  Adieu, Sir.  Seek not to deceive a woman who might have at least some pretensions to your esteem."

Seli-

Selicourt received this epiftle with aftonifhment; for, from the ftyle of it, he guef-
fed, not only that he was lefs indifferent
to the marchionefs than his fears had told
him, but that fhe was even jealous of Madame Darmilli. Vain, however, was his
every effort to procure an interview with her,
till at length Monfieur de Menneville prevailed with her to accompany him to a ball
which was to be given by a lady of her acquaintance. The chevalier failed not to attend; and he had the addrefs to procure admittance to a private apartment into which the
marchionefs, fick of fociety, had retired in
order to give a loofe to her forrows. Her
mafk was off; and fhe difcovered a melting
languor whien gave a new luftre to her
charms. Her hufband had left the rooms,
and was not to return till the clofe of the
night; a circumftance which, by chance,
was known to Selicourt alone, and of which

he omitted not to avail himſelf, by procuring a habit ſimilar to that of Monſieur de Menneville.

"I was afraid," cried he to the marchioneſs as he flew to her in an extaſy; "I was afraid, Madam, of betraying to others the violence of a paſſion which ought not to be known but to yourſelf. My reſpect, you ſee, is equal to my love. Let me beſeech you, therefore, to hear me—to hear me but for one moment, and then deſire me never to ſee you more, deſire me to die, and I will obey you."—

At the recollection of the chevalier's voice, Madame de Menneville felt a thouſand different emotions —felt, that ſhe was no longer able either to fly from him, or to command him from her preſence.

"To obtain one glance of thoſe eyes," continued he, "is, I confeſs it, a happineſs which few, and myſelf leſs than any, deſerve.

ferve.  Yet is my love tender and difinterefted beyond example. To your indifference, however, your hatred I ought perhaps to call it, add not an accufation which would ftamp me the moft bafe, the moft guilty of men. Though I have waited on Madame Darmilli, and have paid thofe compliments to her beauty which beauty deferves, yet have I never once hinted that I love her."——

" Then you love her not?" interrupted the marchionefs, with an agitation which increafed every moment.

" No, Madam," replied the chevalier with warmth, " it is yourfelf alone whom I adore.———Would you permit it, I could eafily juftify myfelf."—

" It is needlefs, Sir.—In what have you offended me ?—I was the firft who advifed

you

you to form an attachment with the baronefs.
She loves you—and I cannot—

She could not utter another word.

" I underſtand you, Madam. You cannot beſtow a ſingle thought upon me. But
does virtue forbid you to eſteem, to pity me?
No: it—but we are obſerved. Suſpicions
may ariſe; and I hold your honour infinitely more dear than either my life or my
love.——Could you expeɕt more of me?
—I take my leave of you with this ſingle
requeſt, that you will permit me once more,
once only, to throw myſelf at your feet, to
unfold to you my heart, to hear you pronounce my deſtiny."——

The marchioneſs could not reſiſt. She
conſented to receive another viſit from Selicourt, upon the expreſs condition, however,
that, from that time, he ſhould for ever
avoid

avoid every place where there was a poſſibility of their meeting. Fully ſenſible of the
value of the permiſſion he had obtained, the
chevalier promiſed an implicit obedience
to her commands ; and the pleaſure he
ſhould feel in ſeeing Madame de Menneville, in telling her, once more, that he
loved her, ingroſſed his ſoul.

How dangerous had ſo much caution, ſo
much reſpect, rendered Selicourt to the
Marchioneſs!

" Ah !"—thought ſhe, abandoning herſelf,
when ſhe had returned home, to a crowd of
thoughts which till then ſhe had been obliged
to ſtifle—" is there a man on earth but Selicourt who is ſuſceptible of a love ſo ardent
and ſo refined ?——How fearful he is to diſ-
oblige me !—— how dear I am to him !——
how deeply he has affected me !——I have
no rival.——It is myſelf, myſelf alone whom

he

he loves.————And may I not return his paſſion without committing an injury to Monſieur de Menneville ?———— No.——— Well then, friendſhip ſhall unite us.——— May not friendſhip ſupply the place of love ? —Friendſhip !—how I ſeek to deceive my-ſelf !————Ought I to give that name to the unhappy tenderneſs by which I am fettered, by which—by which I am ready to be de-ſtroyed ?—Let me *be* deſtroyed rather than yield to it. I have given a promiſe to the chevalier that he ſhould have another inter-view.—I will cancel that promiſe ;—I will ſee him no more, no more betray to him my guilt, my weakneſs and my ſufferings."

And ſhe inſtantly renewed her orders to deny all acceſs to the chevalier.

Selicourt flew to the rendezvous. Ma-dame de Menneville was not at home. He

begged

begged to have admittance, he infifted upon it, and at length prevailed. The marchionefs ftarted back a few fteps in order to avoid him ; but it was in vain, for he was already in her apartment, and determined to oppofe her paffage.

" No, Madam," cried he, " you fhall not fly from me ;—you fhall hear me—hear me for the laft time, if it muft be fo.— Yefterday I facrificed every thing to my delicacy and to your reputation, and to-day, when I have it in my power to fpeak to you without a witnefs, will you deny me audience ?—My fate, Madam, I repeat it to you, is in your hands ;—after this interview, difpofe of me as you will.——Alas ! I have not yet expreffed to what an height I adore you. A paffion like mine deferves not your difpleafure. Nothing can equal my tendernefs for you but my refpect. Not the fmalleft facrifice do I require from you.

In

I loving the moſt valuable of women, the moſt worthy of adoration, will confiſt my happineſs.——Once more let me aſk, what cauſe there can be for alarm in the indulgence of a paſſion which the moſt rigid virtue might permit.—Friendſhip, Madam"—

" Friendſhip !" interrupted the marchioneſs with a deep ſigh, and an earneſt look at the chevalier. —" Why ſhould we deceive ourſelves ?—No, Sir, I ought neither to ſee you nor to liſten to you.——Every moment which I waſte in a converſation, the object of which would unavoidably plunge me into guilt, is a violation of my duty, an inſult to my huſband.—Withdraw, Sir ;—I have already heard too much."—

And ſhe immediately aroſe. Selicourt perceived that ſhe wept.

" What

"What do I fee !" exclaimed he.—"Am I the caufe of thofe tears ?"—

"You are, chevalier," refumed the mar-chionefs, falling back upon her feat, and giving a loofe to her tranfports, " you are the caufe of them."—

"Ah ! Madam—ah ! my charming Men-neville ! are you then, in any degree, af-fected with my fituation ?—do you not hate me ?——

Hate you !—I ought to do it. You have deprived me of my repofe, my tranquillity, my virtue. Now, while her weaknefs is in full difplay before you, take not advantage of an unhappy woman, who is no longer the miftrefs of herfelf, who has loft her reafon, and who beholds her error in its full ex-tent."—

"You

" You have no caufe, fhall have none, to reproach yourfelf," exclaimed the chevalier, fhedding a flood of tears upon the feet of the marchionefs, as he knelt before her.—" Say but that you would love me if your heart was at your difpofal."—

" You wifh then to enjoy your triumph ! —— Do not thefe tears tell you that I would ?"—

And a moment after fhe exclaimed with eagernefs, " Do you love me ?"——

" Love you !—It is not in language to exprefs the fervour with which I adore you."——

" Then I have only to fpeak, to be obeyed ?"——

" You

[ 43 ]

" You have.——To convince you of my
tendernefs, I would think my life a facrifice
too fmall."——

" I require not that you fhould die : — I
require——what I am fenfible is torture to
us both—that you fhould wed Madame Darmilli."——

" Wed Madame Darmilli !"

" Yes, as the ftrongeft teftimony you can
give me of your love.—In confidence fhe has
told me the fecret of her tendernefs for you.
It is in her power to render you happy, chevalier :—render her fo, and—and fee me no
more, forget me."—

" What ! fhall I love the baronefs !—In
the arms of another fhall I—no, Madam, I
will not obey you. Friendfhip, I find, has
mighty influence with you !"—

" It

"It had, till love——how different do I feem from what I was!"——My refolution, Sir, is formed. You muſt either give your hand to Madame Darmilli, or we muſt never fee each other more.——Believe me, it is with no fmall ſtruggle that I reduce you to this alternative.——Yet think not, Selicourt, of what I fuffer.—Exert a becoming firmnefs; reflect that we cannot be united; and be aſſured that the huſband of Madame Darmilli ſhall not ceafe to be the friend of Madame de Menneville."

Hardly had ſhe uttered thefe words, when ſhe flew from the apartment. The feelings of Selicourt upon the occafion are rather to be felt than told.

Though the chevalier often faw Madame Darmilli, yet could he not prevail with himſelf to flatter her with a dawn of hope. Already did ſhe apprehend that ſhe was lefs beloved than

than she had unhappily supposed, already had jealousy stolen a passage into her bosom. Tho' she was unwilling to indulge the smallest suspicion of Madame de Menneville, yet her presence was no longer a pleasure, was troublesome, was even distressing, to her. Notwithstanding his precaution, however, the looks and the sighs which escaped from Selicourt, when he happened to be in company with the two ladies, might have removed every doubt of the baroness, could she have dared to distrust her friend.

Though perhaps it was their wish to avoid each other, yet by the caprice of their fate they perpetually met. One day as they were alone, Madame Darmilli, after a long silence which spoke their mutual perplexity, took occasion to mention the chevalier.

" Do you think that Selicourt loves me?" said the baroness. " I know not whether

my

my fufpicions have any ground, but I cannot help thinking his behaviour cold and
embarraffed.  When I offer to fpeak to him,
he leaves me abruptly :——my very looks he
fhuns.   Yet would I refign every other happinefs for that of receiving his hand,  of giving him all my love, of rendering him the
abfolute mafter of my fortune and of my
heart.—If I had a rival !—I tremble, my dear,
at the thought !"—

Thefe words were fo many mortal ftabs
to the marchionefs.——Her diforder is not
to be conceived.

" What fhall I do ?—Advife me, I beg
of you," continued Madame Darmilli.——
" If I do not marry the chevalier, if he
loves another, I know not, I confefs to
you, what may be the confequence.—Were
that the cafe, there is nothing defperate of

which

which I would not be capable.————With pleafure would I facrifice a life, which"—

" Is he fo very dear to you ?" interrupted Madame de Menneville.

" He is.  It is Selicourt, I own it, who hath taught me to love.————Till the moment, that fatal moment to my repofe, in which I beheld the chevalier, I was the abfolute miftrefs of a heart which is now irrerecoverably his, which is now the feat of forrow and of defpair.  Alas ! I find that I myfelf joined in the deceit.————Why is the chevalier a ftranger to the tendernefs I feel—a tendernefs, which, if I am forced to renounce it, will be more dreadful to me than a thoufand deaths ?—My dear friend, have pity on my weaknefs.————Into your arms I throw myfelf for protection.————To you alone do I open my heart, do I reveal the ftory of my woes."

" What

" What is the matter ?—You weep !"—
continued the baronefs, withdrawing her
hand, upon which Madame de Menneville
had reclined her head, wet with her tears.

" Behold," replied the marchionefs, fobbing as if her heart would burft—" behold
in me a wretch who has facrificed friendfhip,
honour, to love——behold in me your rival,"—

And fhe funk, almoft lifelefs, and drowned in tears, upon a couch.

" Is it you who love Selicourt——you
whom Selicourt loves !——Is it my friend
who betrays me !"—was the only anfwer of
the baronefs. She would have proceeded,
but the words died upon her lips, and fhe
fell down in a fwoon,"—

The

The situation of her friend roused Madame de Menneville into life; and she flew to her assistance. A more affecting scene can hardly be conceived. On opening her eyes, Madame Darmilli, finding herself in the arms of her rival, who wept over her, gave a scream of anguish, and again swooned away. At length she recovered, and started up with horror.

" The veil then is torn from off my eyes ——torn by my rival, the confident of my heart.—I will be revenged."—

" Be revenged," returned Madame de Menneville, throwing herself at her feet, " but let me be the only victim of your fury.——I mean not to extenuate my crime, to appear blameless either in your eyes or in my own. Yet might I plead in my behalf that I urged the chevalier to pay his addresses to you, to accept the honour of your hand, to fly from me, to love me no more.——

" Love you no more !—Then Selicourt loves you !"———

" Hear me," refumed Madame de Menneville, " hear me, and let me receive my punifhment from yourfelf.——I know in what I have offended——know, that I have violated my duty, violated a facred engagement, violated friendfhip. Thefe are crimes for which I muft endeavour to atone. The chevalier fhall never fee me more. If I am dear to him, he fhall pay thofe addreffes to you which I am bound to reject——You fhall know me for your friend," added fhe with a frefh torrent of tears. " It will coft my life, but I fhall have fulfilled my duty, fhall have rendered you happy.———A day will come when you will grieve for me, and do me juftice."——

Wretch

" Wretch that I am !" exclaimed the baronefs.—" Is it you who are the author of
my forrows ?——Dread my fury.——No :
—you are no longer my friend."——

Such was the fituation of thefe unhappy
rivals, fometimes embracing, fometimes with
horror fpurning away each other, fighing,
weeping, when Selicourt entered the room.
He ftopped fhort, ftruck with the fcene.

" It is you, cruel man," cried Madame
Darmilli, running up to him—" it is you
who have reduced us to this diftrefs, who have
plunged a dagger into our bofoms.——Enjoy your triumph in having fet at variance
friends who were moft tenderly united, in
having rendered for ever wretched two women who deferved a better fate."—

The

The chevalier was at no lofs to underftand, that Madame Darmilli had been informed of what he could have wifhed to
have been concealed from her. The grief
of Madame de Menneville pierced his very
heart.

" Yes, Madam," faid he, pointing to the
marchionefs, " from the firft moment that
I beheld that lady, I adored her with a fervour which I feel to increafe every day,
though I know that every thing confpires to
oppofe my happinefs, the fatal knot which
binds her, her virtue—perhaps her indifference"—

" My indifference !" exclaimed Madame
de Menneville.

" For what would you reproach yourfelf?" continued the chevalier.——" You
commanded, that I fhould never fee you
more

more—commanded, that I should make a return to the baronefs for the favourable opinion which she was pleafed to entertain of me.—Madame Darmilli was your conftant theme."—

" I feek not to diffemble my faults," interrupted the marchionefs.—" I have injured my hufband, my friend.——Life is a burthen to me.—Adieu !—Never let us fee each other more.———Deny me not," continued she, turning to the baronefs, " your efteem, your pity.——You have a feeling heart, and can conceive the horror of my fituation.—To heighten it, would ill become Madame Darmil.i."—

And she inftantly withdrew. Selicourt attempted to follow her.

" Stay, Sir," cried the baronefs. " Remember that we are never to fee each other more.

more. Honour, I expect, will enfure your compliance.——No—never let us fee each other more."——

The chevalier fat down, while Madame Darmilli abandoned herfelf to the moft gloomy defpair, to tears and to fobs.

" Thefe tears, thefe fobs, complete my mifery," cried Selicourt.——" I fought not to deceive you in praifing your beauty, your wit.——I was deeply impreffed with gratitude."——

" With gratitude !" interrupted the baronefs.——" Ah ! traitor, what is gratitude compared to what I feel for you ?"——

" It was all I had to give," refumed the chevalier.——" I had feen Madame de Menneville, and my heart was no longer my own. Yet did fhe urge me to devote to you that heart, to form a connection, which, at another

other

other time, would have rendered my happiness complete. In vain did I tell her of my paſſion for herſelf. She inſiſted that I ſhould ſacrifice it to yours; in a word, that I ſhould love, ſhould marry you."—

" 'Tis enough, Sir," replied Madame Darmilli with warmth—" 'tis enough—— leave me—your preſence is hateful to mê— I deteſt you—begone !"—

The baronefs, now ſhe was alone, ſuſtained a thouſand different attacks from grief, from friendſhip, from love, and from deſpair. One moment ſhe would condemn the marchioneſs, the next attempt to juſtify her, and blame herſelf. At certain intervals ſhe reſolved to ſacrifice her paſſion; but Love ſoon returned, ſoon reſumed his empire in her heart.

She

She flew to Madame de Menneville.

" Do you love me ?" faid fhe to her with a faltering voice, after having fat fpeech- lefs for fome time.—" Have I any longer a title to your friendfhip ?"—

" Can you doubt it, my dear baro- nefs ?"

" Then are my life and death in your hands," refumed Madame Darmilli, ftill more agitated, and clafping her rival furi- oufly in her arms. " But tell me pofitively, are you capable of an effort fo great, fo ge- nerous, as that of renouncing for ever your lover for your friend ?——If you again fee Selicourt, I repeat it, my death is certain. I alfo engage never to fee him.——Reflect that, in a fituation like mine, there is no- thing to lofe—reflect"—added fhe in an accent of horror——" that I have it in my

power

power to ruin you.——Your fate, your honour——you underſtand me.——Pronounce then your doom."—

To claſp one of the hands of the baroneſs, and to bathe it with her tears, was all that Madame de Menneville could do.——How lovely did ſhe at that inſtant appear! and to what a pitch of fury did this circumſtance drive Madame Darmilli!

" You anſwer me not but with tears !"—

" What muſt I ſay ?" cried Madame de Menneville.

" That you will follow my example, by never more ſeeing the chevalier."——

" Then you ſhall be ſatisfied.—Be aſſured, that I never will ſee him."—

The

The baronefs retired, and left Madame de Menneville a prey to the moft excruciating forrow.

" Have I then promifed," thought fhe, " never more to behold Selicourt ?—Barbarous woman ! what have you required of me?"—After a number of ftruggles, of heart-felt pangs, fhe determined to acquaint the chevalier of this refolution. She told him in a few words, by letter, that fhe had determined to eradicate every remain of her unhappy tendernefs, and that he muft abfolutely renounce all thoughts of feeing her again. Selicourt, in defpair, wrote feveral letters to the marchionefs, all of which fhe returned to him with the feals untouched. She even avoided all mention of the chevalier to the baronefs ; but the filence of both the ladies in this refpect would perhaps have foon been broken, if Fortune had not removed them to a diftance from each other.

Mon-

Monſieur de Menneville conducted the marchioneſs into the country; where, frequenting the moſt gloomy places, ſhe gave a looſe to her melancholy, and enjoyed from it a pleaſure which love and ſenſibility can alone impart.

" Cruel love!" cried ſhe one day, borne away, as it were, by emotions which ſhe was compelled to repreſs, while ſhe ſat in a ſolitary ſummer-houſe, formed for reflection—" Cruel love! how unhappy haſt thou made me!——In vain do I attempt to extirpate a paſſion which is rooted in my heart.—Selicourt is ſtill before me, ſtill at my feet, vowing eternal love. To friendſhip have I yielded him a ſacrifice.—What do I ſay?—My paſſion was hopeleſs, was frenetic—whither would it have hurried me?"—

" To

" To make me happy without violating your virtue," cried a man, throwing himself at her feet.

Turning round, she beheld Selicourt; and with a shriek she waved her hand to him to retire.

" No," cried he :—" here will I expire, here speak to you, once more, of a love which ought not to have given you pain,— a love which was full of purity and refpect, which taught me to adore you as my supreme divinity."—

At these words he dropped a few tears upon one of the hands of Madame de Men-neville, while he preffed it to his lips.

" Why," added he, " in pronouncing my eternal banifhment from you, did you not

rather

rather pronounce my death ?—Ah ! Madam, will you not beſtow even a look upon me ?—For above this month have I wander-ed through this retreat.—Will you forgive me for the intruſion ?—The idea of being ſo near to you gave me ſome comfort. Often have I beheld you in theſe fields——beheld you, and, when on the point of throwing myſelf at your feet, contented myſelf with adoring you in ſecret. To-day I found my-ſelf no longer capable of that reſtraint, no longer capable of ſeeing you, and not telling you, repeating to you, that nothing can abate my love ; that, to eternity, you ſhall remain the abſolute miſtreſs of my ſoul. In ſome obſcure retreat I am determined to bury myſelf. There will I live alone, to dedicate my every thought to you.—To you I will addreſs my ſighs, my tears, as if you were preſent ; for you, to the very laſt mo-ment, my heart ſhall not ceaſe to beat."—

"Ah !

" Ah ! Selicourt !" exclaimed the marchionefs.

And fhe could not utter another word.
She remained for fome time in filence—but
how expreffive was that filence !—It was the
living picture of love and forrow.

" What do you want, chevalier ?" cried
fhe at length.

" To love you, and to die."—

" Love me !"—Know you not that I am
the wife of Monfieur de Menneville, that I
am the friend of Madame Darmilli, that I
have promifed to her never to fee you more.
—Yet do I fuffer you to remain in my prefence, without commanding you to fly from
me for ever !——Selicourt, an eternal abfence fhall be the confequence of what I am
now about to reveal to you.——I will not
add

add falfehood to weaknefs, by affuming a virtue which I have not.—Know then, that an
unhappy tendernefs had taken root in my
bofom before I knew of yours, that till the
moment I firft beheld you I was a ftranger
to love.—By efteem alone, or rather by the
ties of duty, was I united to Monfieur de
Menneville.——Alas ! you have taught me
how unavailing the dictates of decorum and
of reafon are, when oppofed to the weaknef-
fes of the heart.——You hear then, chevalier, that I loved you ; and perhaps at this
inftant I love you more than ever. Thus
fituated, judge what fteps I ought to take—
judge, whether I ought not to fink under
the weight of my forrows rather than to
give the fmalleft encouragement to a paffion
which renders me criminal in my own eyes.
—I have already told you, Selicourt"——

And her tears burft forth.

"I

.‘‘ I have already told you, that, if I was truly dear to you, you would not fcruple to give your hand to the baronefs. As her hufband, two eternal barriers would be placed between us ; and I might then fometimes fee you, fpeak to you. Efteem would then’’——

‘‘ Hold, Madam,’’ interrupted the chevalier.—‘‘ I am ready to make any facrifice which you may demand of my love ;——it fhall know no bounds when you are to be obeyed. Since you require it, fince your honour and your tranquillity demand it, I will fee you no more.—Myfelf I account as nothing ; death I will embrace : but with a heart, already full of the moft refined, the moft tender paffion, to form a connection with another, to promife to love her, to fupport even the prefence of her, is a degree of felf-command, which is beyond my power.’’—

‘‘ Then

" Then we muſt part," cried the marchioneſs, ſtarting up.——Adieu, chevalier,
—never think of me more."

" Not think of you !—Do you then forbid me to"—

" I expect, Sir, from your tenderneſs,
from your honour, that you will avoid every
opportunity which may bring us together,
that you will inſtantly fly from this place,
that you will leave me——leavé me to expire."—

And the marchioneſs inſtantly withdrew
in tears, while Selicourt with eager eyes followed her to the caſtle.

To deſcribe the ſituation of the chevalier
it were impoſſible. On the ſuppoſition that
his health required it, he retired into a kind
of deſert, at a diſtance from the metropolis.
There, engroſſed by grief and by love,

VOL. II.                    F                    his

his only amufement, his only comfort, was, to weep over, and to gaze upon, a portrait of the marchionefs.

The diftrefs of Madame de Menneville was not lefs poignant. Obliged to confine her forrows within her own bofom, and happy in cherifhing them, it was impoffible to afford relief to her. Yet was the condition of Madame Darmilli more lamentable, perhaps, than that of either the marchionefs or the chevalier. She had not the obftacles of the former to combat; fhe was miftrefs of her hand and of her heart; and fhe was convinced, that, but for Madame de Menneville, fhe would have been beloved by Selicourt: an idea which, every moment that it occurred, rendered her rival odious to her. As friendfhip returned, however, thefe clouds difappeared. Eager to unbofom herfelf, fhe waited upon the marchionefs in the country; who received her with an embar-

rafraſſment which ſhe could not diſſemble, and who, while ſhe ſcrupled not to own that the chevalier had again obtruded himſelf into her preſence, aſſured her that ſhe had renewed her commands to him never to ſee her more.

"No, my dear baroneſs," added ſhe, ſhedding a torrent of tears—" love ſhall not triumph over friendſhip.——I have already given a promiſe to you that it ſhall not, and I will die rather than forfeit that promiſe."—

Madame Darmilli melted.

"Why," cried ſhe, embracing the marchioneſs——" why can I not ſubdue this weakneſs?——Ah! my dear friend, how much are we both to be pitied!—Too long have you ſacrificed yourſelf—now let it be my turn. I am reſolved upon it.—Love the chevalier—let him love you!—What have I ſaid?

ſaid ?—Ah ! cruel woman !—Cruel !—No :
you are my friend, my beſt, my only friend.
—May you be happy !"—

" Happy ! interrupted Madame de Menneville with a deep ſigh—" Can I be happy
in rendering you miſerable, in violating my
duty ? — I have a huſband, and am unpar-
donable if I entertain a thought of a man
but him. —— You know not the extent
of your felicity. Selicourt you may love
—love without remorſe. Fate has decreed
that it ſhould be otherwiſe with me.—But
no more of Selicourt——no more of him,
my friend !"—

The power of the paſſions could not be
more ſtrikingly exhibited than in the conduct of theſe unhappy ladies. Perpetually
did they agree, that neither of them ſhould
mention the chevalier, and perpetually was

the

the chevalier the fubject of their converfation.

They returned to town together. Selicourt, inftead of following them, became
more and more delighted with his retreat.
It feldom happens that a fincere paffion is
unaccompanied with a tafte for folitude.
Pure love is a kind of religious worfhip;
and to feeling hearts how exquifite is the
rapture to be detached from every furrounding object, to give a loofe to, to be engroffed by, thofe fentiments by which they are
captivated, to reflect, that the object of their
love is almoft the fole object of their
thoughts, of their very forrows!——Such
were the pleafures which the chevalier enjoyed. Though deprived of every hope, he
yet ceafed not to vow an eternal attachment
to Madame de Menneville. Thofe grovel-
ing fouls, people of the world, as they are
termed, who are ftrangers to the exceffes of
love,

love, to the charm which accompanies the refinements of it, will pronounce thefe fentiments romantic; but the few who can enjoy a pleafure in the indulgence of their fenfibility, will acknowledge the real, the fubftantial, tranfports of a paffion which in- creafes with time, and which exifts, in fome meafure, by difappointment.

Fortune, however, by an unforefeen event, feemed at length defirous of a reconciliation with Selicourt. Monfieur de Menneville, after an illnefs of fix weeks, was now no more.—What a revolution in the fate of the chevalier!—Hope inftantly fprung up in his bofom; nay, at times, he could not help fuppofing himfelf already the hufband of his adorable marchionefs. Soon as decency would permit, he paid his refpects to her in a letter fraught with tendernefs. The following was her anfwer:

" The

[ 71 ]

" The death of my hufband is an addi-
" tion to my forrows.  While it renders me
" lefs criminal, it renders me perhaps more
" attentive to my conduct.  My heart, I
" am fure, is not changed; but I feel my
" obligation to friendfhip yet more binding
" than ever.  At prefent I do not live; I
" drag on a kind of lingering death, which
" fhall cut fhort my melancholy days ere I
" confent to betray my friend, and hurry
" her into the grave.—Such is our cruel
" deftiny.  At the time that—what was I
" going to fay ?——We muft fubmit.—Let
" us not attempt to fee each other more.
" Your prefence would only heighten my
" diftrefs."


Selicourt was thunder-ftruck.  Hardly
could he believe his eyes.


" What !" exclaimed he twenty times
from the bottom of his heart—" after hav-

ing

ing been the moſt wretched of men, to touch
at the very pinnacle of happineſs, and be, in
a moment, plunged again into the gulph of
ſorrow and of misfortune !—The marchioneſs loves me, ſhe has recovered her liberty
—yet fate forbids that we ſhould unite !”—

His diſtreſs is not to be told, any more
than that of Madame de Menneville.

“ I adore Selicourt,” cried ſhe inceſſant-
ly,—“ I have it in my power to marry him !
—And I have promiſed——promiſed to die
rather than——Ah ! cruel friendſhip, now
art thou ſatisfied ?”—

The very firſt words of the baroneſs to
Madame to Menneville, after the death of
the marquis, were about the chevalier.

“ At

" At length then, my dear," said she, with a look which betrayed her," you are the miftrefs of your heart."—

" I underftand you," replied the mar-chionefs, perhaps equally agitated.—" Yet fear not that I will ever violate my promife."——

And she shed a few tears, which Madame Darmilli either did not fee, or was unwilling to difcover that she did. On the contrary, she defired, she urged, her rival to marry Selicourt.

" How you talk !" exclaimed Madame de Menneville——" Are thefe the fentiments of your heart ?——No : them you attempt to conceal from me——from me who relinquifhes to you what I hold a thoufand times more dear than life.—Know you the value of the facrifice I make to you.—

" My

"My dear Menneville," cried the baronefs, melting into tears, and finking into
the arms of the marchionefs, " you perceive then my weaknefs.—More than ever
does this unhappy, this tyrant paffion opprefs
me.—Too well do I know that I abufe your
generofity.——But will you really be able
to hold your promife, to renounce your happinefs, to deny your hand to the chevalier ?"

" I fhall be able to facrifice every thing
to friendfhip," replied the marchionefs.

And fhe inftantly rufhed from the room,
unable to utter another word.——Madame
Darmilli followed her, called her back, but
in vain. She again waited upon her that very
day, but Madame de Menneville had given
abfolute orders to deny her to all the world.
She would not even receive the letters either
of the baronefs or of Selicourt. Their every
effort was fruitlefs ; and the former ceafed not

to

to bewail the lofs of a friend, whofe company foftened to her the rigours of love, the
latter, to curfe the caprice of his ftars, that
he fhould be loved by the woman he adored
—loved, yet denied all accefs to her prefence.

The baronefs endeavoured to reconcile
herfelf to the abfence of the chevalier;
nay, at times, to perfuade herfelf that her
paffion for him had loft its force. Then it
was that the voice of friendfhip reached to
her heart, that fhe truly pitied the diftrefs
of the marchionefs.

" Ah ! Madam," cried Selicourt, rufhing
one day into the apartment of Madame Darmilli, and throwing himfelf at her feet—"'my
all is at ftake, and you alone can affift me.—
Save, fave your friend, and I will return
and die at your feet."—

" What

" What is the matter, Sir ?"—

" The marchionefs, Madam, I am told,
is feized with a dreadful illnefs. It proceeds
—doubt it not—from her generous ftruggles
to fubdue a paffion, which—which is offenfive to you.—From your virtue, from your
magnanimity, I expect that you will inter-
pcfe ; and be affured, that the powers of
friendfhip and of gratitude over me are infinite."—

" Ah ! Selicourt, they can never equal
thofe of love."——

And fhe inftantly ordered her carriage.

" Come, chevalier, your hand."—

They drove to the houfe of Madame de
Menneville ; and notwithftanding every order which had been given to the contrary,
they

they procured accefs. Selicourt remained in
an antichamber, while the baronefs advanced to the room of the fick lady.

The marchionefs was in reality in a dangerous condition. Her head was reclined
upon her hand ; and from her large black
eyes, rendered yet more affecting by a dead-
ly languor, flowed a rivulet of tears, which
fpoke the anguifh of her heart. —— At
the fight of her rival, fhe could not reftrain
a fhriek.

" Let not my prefence," cried the baro-
nefs, " give the fmalleft uneafinefs to you.
—Behold in me a friend, whofe only ambi-
tion is, to contribute to your happinefs.—
For that purpofe am I now come hither.
Too long have we abufed friendfhip.——
Henceforth let that give way to love.——
Now that you are the miftrefs of your heart
and perfon, let me infift, that you will be-
ftow

flow both upon Selicourt.——Come in," continued Madame Darmilli, as the marchioness was about to anfwer—" come in, chevalier.——I prefent to you, my dear, a lover, whofe fteady attachment amply entitles him to your hand——foon may he enjoy it !——Regard not my tears :—they are the laft effufions of a paffion, which—— which I will overcome.——At prefent, I feel not a wifh but to recall you, my dear marchionefs, to life, and to fee you happy with the man of your heart."—

Selicourt threw himfelf upon his knees before the marchionefs, clafped one of her hands, and covered it with kiffes and with tears.

" For exerting your influence with Madame de Menneville to accept of my homage," faid he, turning to the baronefs, " I fhall ever confider you, madam, as my

greateft

greateſt benefactreſs, as an unexampled friend. The marchioneſs alone will I love with greater tenderneſs."—

"'Tis enough, Sir," interrupted Madame de Menneville haſtily.— "Generous friend !" added ſhe, addreſſing herſelf to the baroneſs.——" Well do you deſerve that name. What pleaſure does it give me to find how dear I am to you, to find that I am not unworthy of ſuch noble, ſuch diſintereſted, friendſhip !——My happineſs, baroneſs, ſhall not be eſtabliſhed at the expence of yours :——your heart ſhall not be torn that mine may be reſtored to life. Without a breach of decorum, I may now avow, that I love the chevalier, that he has inſpired me with ſentiments which will not periſh but with my life. Remember, however, our engagement to each other— remember, that if one of us is happy, the other muſt be miſerable. A thouſand

deaths,

deaths, I own it, would I suffer, if you were to marry Selicourt; and I am perfuaded that if I should be so perfidious, so cruel, as to give my hand to him, I should dig a grave for you.——Our doom then is pronounced."——

And she turned to the chevalier.

" Is it thus, Sir, that you keep your promife?—What charms can you find in the fight of two women, whom you have diftracted ?—I pleafed myfelf in thinking you a model of fenfibility.——Away !——Away from us for ever !——Pity our weaknefs, and be fatisfied with having robbed us both of quiet, and me of life."——

The baronefs had funk into the arms of her friend——Selicourt was ftill at her feet. The former renewed with warmth her folicitations in behalf of the chevalier; and

after

after a long and a dreadful conflict, love triumphed, and the marchioneſs conſented to become the wife of Selicourt. She ordered him to conduct Madame Darmilli home.

"You cannot," added ſhe, " ſhew ſufficient gratitude to our generous friend.——She deſerves to be adored.——Let her then partake with me of your tenderneſs—I ſhall not be jealous."—

And ſhe again embraced the baroneſs, as ſhe withdrew with the chevalier.

" Well," ſaid Madame Darmilli to him, eying him with attention, the moment they were alone—" well, Sir, now are you contented?—Is it in woman to do more than I have done?"—

The acknowledgments of Selicourt were acccompanied with an air of embarraſſment; and he attempted to quit the baroneſs, whoſe agitation encreaſed every moment.

"You ſhall not leave me, Sir," cried ſhe, running to him :——"you ſhall ſtay—ſtay to receive my laſt ſighs."—

And with a flood of tears ſhe ſunk back upon a chair.

"What do I ſee, Madam ?"——

"My death, cruel man——my death, which will ſoon put a period to my woes.— Alas! it is not in my power to conceal that I never loved you to ſuch an height as now. —Your happineſs will coſt me my life.—— Let it.—Ah! chevalier, behold not a ſor- row, a deſpair, for which I am myſelf a- ſhamed.——Go to the altar ; marry Madame

de

de Menneville; give to her all your tendernefs——never think of me.——Yet, un-.
grateful man, will you not pity me ?——
Alas ! what is pity in return for the feelings
with which I am tortured !——Once more
let me intreat, that you will never fee me,
liften to me, more.—I am the moft wretched
of women."—

Sobs choked her utterance, while Selicourt traverfed the apartment with a preci-
pitation which powerfully exprefled his diftraction.

" Can a heart feeling as yours is," cried
he, throwing himfelf in tears at her feet,
and taking hold of one of her hands, " be
a ftranger to the fweets of friendfhip !——
Every day will I fee you—every day will I
repeat to you, that you are my benefactrefs,
my friend, my generous friend, that I owe
every thing to you."—

" Ah !

" Ah ! chevalier, friendſhip is not love.
—Go, I tell you, leave me to all the horrors of my fate.  Think not of aught but
the pleaſure of loving Madame de Menneville.—Death cannot come too ſoon to my
relief."——

Selicourt ſtarted up with fury.

" This is too much, Madam.  I ſhall find
a way to ſatisfy you, to atone to you for a
love, which is the ſource of ſo much ſorrow
to you.  My happineſs ſhall not be purcha-
ſed at the expence of your life.—This inſtant
will I put a period to an exiſtence which
is become a burden to me."—

Already was his drawn ſword at his
breaſt.

Ma-

Madame Darmilli, with a fhriek, flew to prevent him, turned afide the weapon, and pointed it to her own heart.

" Let me perifh !" exclaimed fhe.—Cruel
" man !—and would you oppofe my refolution ?—Let loofe my arm.—Know you not
how dear you are to me, how unavailing my
days are when weighed with yours ?—Live—
live to forgive me. I repeat it to you, that I
am fully fenfible of my guilt in giving way
to fuch tranfports. But, chevalier, you
love, and can be no ftranger to the extravagances of a hopelefs paffion—a paffion which
is rejected and defpifed.———I am not, never
fhall be, beloved !—Henceforth will I ftem
my tears, will I give the law to my heart.
This is the laft time that you fhall ever behold
thefe difgraceful conflicts.—By the help of
reafon and of time, I fhall recover my tran-
quil-

quillity, my virtue.——You weep!—Ah! how affecting are thefe tears!—No longer, Selicourt, will I importune you with complaints which are equally diftreffing to us both.—All I afk is, that you will refpect my weaknefs, and that you will conceal from Madame de Menneville to what a pitch I have betrayed her friendfhip.——Alas! why can I not conceal from myfelf that I am actuated by emotions which are equally humiliating to my vanity and to my honour? —My reafon, my pride, my virtue, are no more. By one unhappy paffion is my foul engroffed.—That I will contend with, will conquer. Have pity on an unfortunate woman, whofe—whofe only refource is in death."—

The chevalier could not prevail with himfelf to leave Madame Darmilli. Having affured him that fhe would herfelf urge the marchionefs to haften their union, he at length withdrew, almoft convinced that the baro-

nefs

nefs would be enabled to effect her generous purpofe.

The day appointed for the happinefs of the chevalier now approached. On the receipt of a billet from the marchionefs, requefting an interview with him for one moment, he flew to her on the wings of impatience.

"Sit down, chevalier," faid fhe to him the inftant he appeared;—"I have fomething to fay to you upon a point which is more ferious than you perhaps imagine.—— You are well affured that I love you, that I would do every thing in my power to accelerate our union. Far from blufhing for a paffion fo pure and fo worthily placed, I am happy in fhewing you that I partake of your impatience. The hour is now nearly come in which I ought to enjoy the fatisfaction of calling you hufband. Selicourt, was there

ever

ever fenfibility like mine ?——To that fenfibility alone it is owing that our happinefs
has been fo long, and muft be ftill, delayed."—

" What do I hear ?—Delayed !"

" Selicourt, do you love me ?"—

" Love you ! Ah ! Madam, it is not in
language to exprefs with what rapture I doat
on you."—

" I believe you, chevalier——then hear
what I have to fay.——The more that my
friend endeavours to difguife from me the
horrors of her fituation, the more ought I to
partake of them.—Reflect that it is on our
account fhe fuffers, on our account fhe
dies."—

" Why

" Why, Madam, not a day elapfes in
which fhe fpeaks not to me of our marriage,
in which fhe tells me not that our happinefs will be hers."—


" Selicourt, fhe deceives you—alas ! deceives herfelf.—She imagines that fhe is cured
of a paffion, of which fhe is more and more
the unhappy victim.—Believe me, I am no
ftranger to the effects of love.—The torture
of the baronefs is rendered yet more intolerable by her filence.—Let us then attempt to
alleviate her woes. From your tendernefs,
I expect a compliance with what I now requeft of you.—Your relations in the country, who love you, and whom you love,
wifh to fee you :——retire then to them,
and"—


" Can you be fo cruel, Madam, as to
exact fuch a facrifice of me ?—In your heart
then

then the influence of love is feeble to that of friendſhip !"—

It is not, Selicourt :—every delay ſeems to heighten my tenderneſs for you. But it is the duty of us both to ſubmit to this cruel trial. Virtue commands that we ſhould ;——and would you have our love to be inconſiſtent with virtue ?—Let us then exert a reſolution to ſupport an abſence which will ſerve to endear us to each other yet more. Go, but ſee not Madam Darmilli, think not of what I ſuffer. When the favourable moment for your return arrives, I will inform you. Then ſhall we be united in bands that are indiſſoluble."——

The chevalier ſat ſpeechleſs with ſorrow. He threw himſelf at the feet of the marchio-neſs, preſſed one of her hands to his lips, and bathed it with his tears.

"You

" You love me," exclaimed he at length, ſtarting up—" I breathe but for you, yet you charge me to fly from you !"—

The ſituation of Madame de Menneville was equally to be pitied. Selicourt, obedient to her commands, immediately left Paris. Then, abandoning herſelf to all the bitterneſs of ſorrow, did ſhe accuſe herſelf of barbarity, did ſhe call aloud for her lover, did ſhe even blame him for his compliance with her will. On the day before that which had been appointed for her marriage, ſhe received a viſit from the baroneſs, who in vain attempted to conceal the exceſs of her anxiety. A ghaſtly paleneſs overſpread her cheeks ; and ſhe could only utter, with a faltering voice, " To-morrow then you crown the wiſhes of Selicourt !"—

And ſhe rivetted her eyes upon Madame de Menneville.

" What

" What is the matter ?" continued she.—
" You weep !"——

" No," anfwered the marchionefs in a
firm tone :—" I do not weep, Madam.—Be
eafy—I fhall not marry Selicourt."—

" What do I hear ?"—

" Hear !—that to friendfhip I have made
a facrifice of love ; that I have banifhed Selicourt into the country, till yourfelf fhall
urge me to call him hufband."—

Tranfported with gratitude and with admiration, the baronefs embraced the knees
of her friend.

" Ah ! Marchionefs," exclaimed fhe,
" what difinterefted friendfhip !——what a
noble effort !—Is it poffible that for me you
could

could relinquiſh every thing that ought to be moſt dear to you."—

Madame de Menneville eagerly raiſed her rival, and preſſed her to her boſom.

" What then," cried the latter, " ſhall we never more ſee Selicourt ?"—

" That muſt depend upon you," replied the marchioneſs.

" But, my dear friend," reſumed Madame Darmilli, " is it indeed true that my heart rebelled, that your marriage"— .

" My marriage," interrupted Madame de Menneville abruptly, " would have planted a thouſand daggers in your boſom.—I love the chevalier, and I know every torture which I ſhould feel if he were to beſtow his hand upon a woman but myſelf."—

" My

" My adorable friend," exclaimed the baronefs, throwing herfelf at the feet of Madame de Menneville, " from my tears alone can you conceive my feelings.—How much am I indebted to you !—How mean, how guilty, do you render me to myfelf ! ——You fhew me my weaknefs and my faults, in their utmoft extent. —— You force me to confefs to you, what I wifhed to conceal even from myfelf—to confefs, that I love the chevalier ftill.——Alas ! inftead of pitying me, call me the moft perfidious, the moft barbarous, of friends.—No: rather help me to deceive myfelf.——Tell me that my heart is free, and by the power of your perfuafions I fhall myfelf perhaps be convinced that it is fo.—Marchionefs, I will myfelf recall Selicourt, will myfelf conduct him to the altar. —Your happinefs I will efteem my own."—

Ah ! my dear baronefs, you promife too much. Give me but your word that you will fupport the fight, and I afk no more.—But, in your fituation, what are promifes!—Life we may throw off, but love!—No, my friend: wounds like yours, are not to be cured but by time.—Till you have recovered the empire of your heart, therefore, I will wait.—Meanwhile let us engage, that, in the prefence of each other, even the name of Selicourt fhall not efcape from us."—

" Not even his name !"—

" By banifhing the very remembrance of the chevalier can we alone recover that ferenity, which is abfolutely neceffary for us both before we determine upon his return.—On this condition only, my dear, let us fee each other.——

The promifes of Madame Darmilli were unbounded; yet would they have been per-

petually

petually violated but for the affiduity of the marchionefs, in turning from their converfation every circumftance which might tend to introduce the chevalier. Poorly was fhe rewarded by the numberlefs letters of her lover. In thefe he failed not to dwell upon his conftancy, his defpair, while fhe anfwered him with hopes of what, in her heart, fhe knew to be ungrounded. Even by jealoufy were her tortures heightened. True love cannot reconcile itfelf to abfence, is a ftranger to fecurity, and is ever open to fufpicion, whofe recoil, like that of a dart which is concealed, it is impoffible to prevent.

"At length you fhall be fatisfied with your friend," cried Madame Darmilli to her, one day, as fhe fat abforbed in forrow.——" I am reftored to reafon.—I have carefully examined my heart, and am convinced of it."—

The

The marchionefs looked at her.

" Yes, my dear friend, I can now fpeak to you of Selicourt without emotion.   He fhall return, you fhall give him your hand."—

" Can I believe you ?—This change is"—

" For life, my dear," interrupted the baronefs.—" No longer am I enflaved by a paffion, which facrificed every thing to itfelf,. which to you was the fource of fo much forrow, to myfelf, of reproach."—

" Then you no longer love the chevalier ?"—

" Love him !—No :— friendfhip has at length prevailed.——My fentiments are now pure and difinterefted.——If I do love Selicourt, it is no longer for my own fake, but for

his.————I have not a wish but for his happinefs.————With what pleafure fhall I again
behold him, fhall I tell him to what an height
my tendernefs"——


" Ceafe, my friend," interrupted Madame de Menneville.———" There is more
danger in thofe fentiments than you imagine."—


" It is impoffible.————My victory is
complete.———Would you have a proof of
it?————You fhall, in a letter to Selicourt."——


" To Selicourt!"—


" Yes: and now will I write it under
your eye."—


Having rung for ink and paper, fhe immediately writ an epiftle to the chevalier,
ftrongly

ſtrongly urging him to return. Hardly had ſhe ſealed and addreſſed it, when another viſitor was announced to the marchioneſs. Madame Darmilli withdrew ; and on her return to her apartment her every ſenſe forſook her, and ſhe fell down in a ſwoon. On opening her eyes ſhe found herſelf in bed, and ſurrounded with her attendants. Theſe, with a torrent of tears from the bottom of her very heart, ſhe ordered to retire.

" And have I ſo far deceived myſelf !" exclaimed ſhe, giving a vent to her tears.— " Have I recalled Selicourt—recalled him to the arms of my rival, at a time too when I adore him more than ever !—Wretch that I am, I have impoſed upon the marchioneſs—impoſed upon myſelf.——The marchioneſs is not my friend.——My friend !— Can I doubt that ſhe is not ?—No longer then let me be a bar to her felicity.——

Men-

Menneville fhall not know of my diftraction :—fooner will I die than betray to her
my guilty weaknefs."—

Madame Darmilli had in reality not only
the refolution to difguife her diftrefs from
the marchionefs, but even the addrefs to
convince her, that fhe had actually triumphed
over her paffion.

Soon as the chevalier had received the
letter, he flew to Madame de Menneville.
Eager to exprefs his gratitude to Madame
Darmilli, he waited upon her alfo, and was
denied admittance. In the fear of betraying
herfelf, the unhappy baronefs had recourfe
even to ftratagem. She wrote a letter to
the marchionefs, acquainting her that a family bufinefs called her into the country for
a few days, preffing her to conclude her marriage, and promifing that fhe would return to Paris to affift at the ceremony.
Both

Both Madame de Menneville and Selicourt concluded, that she was in reality interested in their happiness, and desirous to witness it. They wrote repeatedly to her, and her answers confirmed them in this opinion. At length the day of their union was announced to her. It came, and Madame Darmilli did not appear. The marchioness desired to wait till her arrival; but the chevalier was impatient, and love was too powerful for the scruples of his bride.

Selicourt was intoxicated with his happiness. Something, however, was still wanting to complete that of Madame de Menneville; and the following letter from the baroness again overwhelmed her in sorrow:

"All is over then. I have seen every thing ——— have seen you bestow your hand upon Selicourt. My misery is confirmed. Tremble when I inform you of the

dangers

dangers which threatened you, of the horrid extravagances which I was upon the point of committing. It avails not now to conceal from you the fituation of my heart;—I am myfelf frightened at it. You are not to be told that every effort has been exerted to eradicate my unhappy paffion; that with my life I would have atoned for it. At times, I imagined that it was enfeebled, and that at length reafon would completely deftroy it.——Alas! I deceived you, deceived myfelf.——Too well am I now convinced that I did. Never was I more weak, more criminal, more wretched than I am at this moment.—— Triumph, cruel pair—enjoy my forrow.——Yes, Selicourt, every day art thou more dear to me :—with my laft figh will I pronounce thy name.——Hardly had I written that fatal letter to the chevalier when my tyrant love returned, and every fenfe forfook me. With new efforts did I attempt to banifh it. That I might not be

expofed

expofed to the view of the author of
my woes, and that I might not retard
your marriage, I feigned a journey into the
country.   Yet was I anxious to behold the
completion of thofe woes.   Unfeen amidft
the crowd, I followed you to the church.
There, with my eyes riveted on Selicourt
and you, was I racked with a thoufand different emotions, did I form a thouſand different projects.   In the firft tranfports of
my fury, I was on the point of rufhing to
the altar, of ftabbing to the heart Selicourt,
you, myfelf.   Let me acknowledge the good-
nefs of heaven in averting my horrid purpofe.——Adieu.——Never more fhall I importune you with a recital of my forrows.—
How weak is the human heart!——How
powerful are the paffions!—In the moft ob-
fcure retreat, far from your knowledge, will
I bury myfelf:——there is no grave deep
enough to hide me."

For

For years, but in vain, did Madame de Menneville and her hufband perfift in their enquiries after the baronefs. Her fufferings ceafed not to engrofs the thoughts of the marchionefs, and to embitter all her joys. Even the birth of two children availed not to her happinefs. One day, as Selicourt and fhe were talking of their unhappy friend, and fhedding a tear to her memory, an unknown lady from the country was announced to them. She entered; and, at the fight of Madame Darmilli, they inftantly fhrieked.

" At length," cried the baronefs, rufhing into their arms—" at length you embrace a real friend.——I am not deceived as to my fentiments now; they are thofe of the moft exalted friendfhip."—

They loaded Madame Darmilli with careffes; and, in anfwer to their enquiries,

fhe

ſhe thus related her adventures ſince their ſeparation.

"  I need not," ſaid the baroneſs, " deſcribe to you either my weakneſs or my diſtreſs at the time of your marriage :—well do you know the extent of both. Tired of life, and afraid to die, I wandered from province to province under a borrowed name. I changed my abode, but could not change my heart —— could not baniſh my grief, my love, my deſpair. At length I arrived at an obſcure village, conſiderably diſtant from Grenoble. There I took a houſe, and lived ſecluded from all ſociety but that of a faithful maid, who was the confidant of my ſorrows. An aged gentleman, who had formerly ſerved in the army, of famed probity and benevolence, hearing, as he has ſince informed me, of my melancholy, and deſirous, by his counſels and his company, to remove it, begged leave to wait upon me. I received him with a cold politeneſs which

was

was rather a difcouragement to his future vifits. Thefe, however, Sinville — fo my venerable friend is called—ftill continued ; and by degrees he gained my confidence. To him I unfolded all my forrows, and by him I have been enabled to put an end to them. Aided by his reflections, I turned my eyes upon the objects of this world, and beheld that all was fallacy ; that we were in perpetual fearch of a happinefs from others, which was not to be found but in ourfelves. From earth I raifed my eyes to heaven. Then did my chriftian philofopher inforce to me, with equal wifdom and perfuafion, that God alone ought to be the object of our affections, of all our pleafures and of all our pains.—That he is our only comforter, I have thoroughly experienced.—Behold then your rival," continued fhe, addreffing herfelf to Selicourt.—" He has been fuccefsful, and has eradicated from my bofom every fentiment for you but what Reafon dictates, and Virtue blufhes

· blushes not to own.——The marchionefs," she added, with an agreeable fmile, " will have no caufe to be jealous of him.—But I muft introduce you to my guide. Together we quitted our retreat, and together we will return to it. Convinced that you were interefted in my fate, I could not be eafy till I had informed you of this happy change."—

Madame de Menneville again fprung into the arms of her friend, again loaded her with careffes, while, with tears, she recounted what she had herfelf fuffered during her abfence.

The baronefs prefented Sinville to them, and he immediately became one of their party. The piety of this worthy man was untinctured with a forbidding aufterity. He gave to virtue charms infinitely fuperior to thofe of worldly wfidom. Upon his face fat an inviting fmile of gaiety, which fpoke the ferenity of his foul, and banifhed every wrinkle. The

cries

cries of the unfortunate never reached him in vain. His bounty was without oftentation, as his virtue was without arrogance. He was unwilling to fuppofe that he was more deferving than his neighbour; and in all his actions he was not more biaffed by duty than by inclination.

Qualities fo valuable could not fail to render him every day more dear to Selicourt and to the marchionefs. They invited both him and the baronefs to continue in Paris, and to live with them. Madame Darmilli would have chofen to continue with her old friends, but Sinville declined the offer. He infifted, that with the very air of a town, we breathe, in fome meafure, frivolity and corruption; that to be truly virtuous, a time muft be fet apart for an enquiry into ourfelves; and that in retirement alone we have it in our power to fow the feeds of a happy difpofition, and to make them flourifh. He was of opinion

that

that fociety is productive of infinitely more evils than of bleffings and advantages. "How many men," faid he, " are loft in the crowd of a capital, and can hardly be faid to exift, who might have acted up to the dignity of their being, if they had poffeffed the refolution to continue in the country !"——He thought as did that Englifhman, who compared the diffipated French to a medal, whofe impreffion, defaced by friction, can no longer be diftinguifhed. The venerable man agreed, however, to return, once a year, with the baronefs, and to pafs a few months with them. This promife he faithfully performed ; and thefe valuable friends became every day more ftrongly attached to the practice of virtue, and to the fweets of genuine love.

[illegible]
[illegible]
[illegible]
[illegible]
[illegible]
[illegible]
[illegible]
[illegible]
[illegible]
[illegible]
[illegible]
[illegible]
[illegible]
[illegible]
[illegible]
[illegible]
[illegible]

# SIDNEY and SILLI;

## OR, THE

## MAN OF BENEVOLENCE,

### AND THE

## MAN OF GRATITUDE.

# SIDNEY and SILLI;

## OR, THE
## MAN of BENEVOLENCE,
### AND THE
## MAN of GRATITUDE.

I WAS at Slaughter's coffee-houfe the other day, as ufual; when, after having difcuffed the moft profound political fub-jeɛts, we began to difcourfe of philofophy and philofophers. Some of us declared for Bacon, fome for Locke; but the majority agreed, that of the fages of England, Newton was the chief.

A lufty gentleman, who had liftened to us with a kind of critical indifference, and who had almoft choaked us with tobacco fmoke, laid down his pipe, and calmly ad-dreffed himfelf to us.

<table><tr><td>I 2</td><td>"Gen-</td></tr></table>

" Gentlemen," faid he, " you have not the fmalleft idea of wifdom and philofophy. A philofopher, according to my conception, is he who promotes the happinefs of mankind, not one of thofe crack-brains who become martyrs to their chimerical fyftems. I deny not that Sir Ifaac is a great man, yet I know one ftill greater than him."—

With thefe words, he refumed his pipe, and continued to fmoke with the fame dignity.—His laft affertion excited our curiofity.—A greater man than Newton! thought we.——Who can be this extraordinary mortal?——

We advanced towards the fmoker; and one of the company politely begged of him to inform us who it was that excelled this prince of Englifh philofophers, this glory of his nation.

" That

" That I will with pleafure," replied he:—" I am delighted when I behold public homage given to virtue; and I doubt not but that my fage will be yours.—Here, waiter !—Bring us a bottle of port.—Port, gentlemen, is excellent to moiften converfation."—

The franknefs of the ftranger charmed us. We alfo ordered fome wine; and, having feated ourfelves round the table, we urged him to begin his narrative.

" With all my heart, gentlemen," faid he; after having fwallowed a large bumper; " and I prefume I fhall make you acquainted with the character of a true philofopher;— a character, which is fo often falfely affumed, that I declare I am quite difgufted with all thofe differtations upon your phenomena of pedantry.——Zounds!" (and he fhook his pipe with violence) " it is not in writing

books

books that virtue fhines :—it is in perform-
ing worthy actions, in rendering ourfelves
ufeful to our fellow-creatures, in confoling
them amidft their misfortunes."—

This preamble ftill heightened our attention.

" Such as you fee me," continued he,
" I have read, like other men, a number
of ferious follies, and have filled my head
with a thoufand fplendid nothings called
Notions. I have travelled, and feen an
infinite number of dwarfs, who thought
themfelves men, of fools, who pronounced themfelves fages.———After hawing
twice made the tour of the world, I
met in India with an Englifh gentleman,
named Sidney. He was in the land-fer-
vice; and though rich, yet he was a ftranger to the rigour of pride: a character
more fimple, and more modeft, never exifted. I formed a connection with my
worthy

-worthy countryman. Every day did I difcover in him fome new virtue, which he
rendered yet more refpectable by his endeavours to conceal it. But, to come to my
ftory, I will pafs over a multiplicity of
circumftances, every one of which would
form an illuftrious eulogium. What I am
now about to relate of our fellow-citizen was
told me by one of his intimate friends; for
Sidney never yet blazed forth to the world
his own benevolent actions. You will not
be furprifed at the exactnefs of my narrative,
when I inform you, that, having already
written it with my own hand, I know it by
heart. It is more worthy of that trouble,
in my opinion, than all the pretended at-
chievements of your Cefars and your Alex-
anders, which we imprefs upon our me-
mories with fo much care, and with fo
little advantage.

Sidney enjoyed in India a military employment of the firft diftinction. We were
then

then at war with a Nabob; and during a rencounter, from which we came off victorious, there appeared among the natives an European who fought with fury, and who, having rushed upon the English battalions, had slain several men, and was covered with blood. In the instant that he attracted the eyes of our countryman, he vented his rage upon a soldier, who expired under him. This bloody deed excited in Sidney a degree of surprise hardly inferior to his indignation. That there must be some uncommon cause for it he was convinced; and he gave orders that the man should be seized, and brought to him alive. The troops accordingly fell upon him; and with much trouble they at length tore him from his prey, and carried him, deprived of his senses by the loss of blood, to the tent of their general. On advancing towards him, in order to examine his features, Sidney perceived that they were noble and engaging, that they

were

were expreffive of a generous foul; and he knew not how to accord the vifage of the ftranger with that fpirit of fury which had animated him in the field.

" Unhappy young man !" exclaimed Sidney, gazing upon him—" is it poffible thou canft have a countenance thus affect-ing, and a foul thus barbarous, thus in-human ?—Whence can fpring fo unnatural a contraft ?"

The wounds of the prifoner were care-fully dreffed ; and at length he opened his eyes.

" To behold again the light of day !"— cried he—" to be furrounded by men, and be unable to pluck out their hearts !—O my God, my God !"—

And he fprung up. Prefently, however, he fell back, clofed again his eyes, and

attempted

attempted to tear off the bandages which had been applied to his wounds. From accomplishing this he was prevented by his attendants ; and he fainted away a second time. The concern he had excited in the bofom of 'Sidney encreafed. He gave ftrict charge, that proper care fhould be taken of him, and that he fhould be informed when he had recovered from the lethargic ftupor, in which his fenfes were now overwhelmed.

" This man," faid he, " muft be oppreffed by fome violent paffion, by fome dreadful misfortune, to hold mankind in fuch abhorrence.—His rage is unnatural.—The human heart, of itfelf, is incapable of cruelty in fuch excefs."—       .

Prompted by the prepoffeffion he had conceived in his favour, Sidney prefently returned. Hardly had he appeared, when the ftranger, raifing his dying eye-lids,

again

again endeavoured to pull off his bandages.
Sidney feized his hands.

" What are you doing, Sir?" cried he.—
" You are not among Savages:—the Englifh
are Men."——

" Men!" replied the other with a gloomy
defpair.—" Thefe are the monfters I would
deftroy.—If you retain one fpark of pity
among you, if you are not actually lions, tigers, fuffer me to die:—it is the only comfort
I wifh for, fince it is denied me to deftroy, to
drag with me to the grave, the whole human
race.——O heaven! put a period to my
horrible exiftence!——Your efforts, Sir,
are vain," added he, addreffing himfelf to
Sidney.—" Notwithftanding your perfidious fuccour, I fhall find means to procure
death—death, which, to me, will be the
firft of bleffings."——

With thefe words he funk back upon his pillow, and gave a vent to a few fobs.

This fpectacle melted yet more the tender heart of our countryman.—The moft affectionate parent could not do more for his child than did Sidney for his prifoner.

By degrees, and as if againft his will, the wounded youth was reftored to life. Often did he groan, and often was he feen to fhed thofe tears which feeling fouls, who can diftinguifh the different impreffions of grief, know to be the tears of the heart. The unwearied attention of Sidney affected him.

" Is it poffible then," faid he to him, during an interval in which he appeared rather compofed—" is it poffible, that you are a man, and yet poffefs not a heart of iron ?—Alas! do you think I am capable of gratitude ?—

ude?—What hope can you entertain of it?—Why preserve a life which is a source to me of the most bitter calamities?—Ah! let me die—let me die, since, at length, I have found that there is benevolence on earth."——

"What!" replied Sidney—"will you not love me?—I am an Englishman; you seem to be a Frenchman—but there can be no enemy in the heart of Sidney.—Sidney will alleviate your sorrows:—he is the friend of the unhappy."—

"Does there then a friend exist!—Alas! Sir, I have lived too long—You have beheld my fury—beheld my cruel hatred of Man.—It was Man who taught me barbarity—who"—

And a torrent of tears choaked his utterance.

"I am

" I am not, Sir, a barbarian, a monſter:—
I am endowed with fenſibility—yes, with a
fenſibility, which has been my bane."—

Sidney embraced him.

" Come, young man," cried he, " have
courage :—my foul is open to you.—I doubt
not that this ferocity is foreign to your
diſpoſition :—I ſaw that it was in your features, tinged as they were with blood."—

" Indeed, Sir, I am far from being inhuman.—Conceive my deſpair, ſince they
could force me ſo far to debaſe myſelf, ſo
far to renounce my very nature.——I abhor
myſelf.——O Man! unworthy art thou
of the name—how was I formed to love
thee!——

" But, dear Sir, where have you lived ?—
Among the monſters of the foreſts ?"——

" Would

' " Would to heaven I had !——No, Sir : I lived among Men—I lived in the heart of Paris."——

Thus by degrees did the generous Sidney lead him to the recital of his misfortunes.

But come, gentlemen, allow me to help you to a glafs of wine, and to drink one myfelf.—Give ear, and you fhall be acquainted with my Sidney—be acquainted with a true philofopher.

The captive ftranger raifed himfelf, and leaned upon one arm.

" You feem, Sir," cried he, " to be worthy of my confidence.—Hear then my juftification—hear my diftreffes, and judge if my deteftation of life, my deteftation of mankind, is ungrounded.——

" I was

" I was born in Paris, of parents who were natives of a province where the nobles are poorly befriended by Fortune. My father had come thither in order to make application at court for a commiſſion in the army; and after much trouble, and many rebuffs, he ſucceeded. He had married a young lady of rank, whoſe virtue and beauty were equally conſpicuous. Of ſeveral children I am the oldeſt. One of my brothers periſhed in the field; a circumſtance, which my mother did not long ſurvive, leaving my father with one ſon and one daughter, and with little or nothing as a proviſion for them.

" I will not dwell upon my infant years, though they were diſtinguiſhed by a ſenſibility which has been the ſource of all my misfortunes, of all my ſorrows. Tenderneſs and humanity, the characteriſtics of my ſoul, were pictured on my countenance. I

was

was educated in the principle that virtue, probity, and fenfibility, were the fteps to happinefs; that men were obliging, and ready to comfort, to affift, their fellow-creatures. Hardly had I quitted my cradle when I contracted a fondnefs for books. It was in thefe deceitful mirrors that I examined the human character, that I beheld heroes, fages, beheld hearts of benevolence, and friends of fidelity—in a word, beheld, that there were Men ; and my foul delighted to open to, and to be engroffed by, the dear illufion.

'Thus I thought, or rather thus I felt, on my entrance into the world. My birth ; fome tafte I happened to poffefs for thofe chimeras they call the Fine Arts—which, though with the generality of men, it only ferves to extinguifh fentiment, yet kept it alive, and cherifhed it, in me—my wifh to pleafe; a certain neceffity I felt of loving every object around me—in a word, my candour—

thefe were the advantages with which I engaged in fociety; and I put fome value
upon them. I foon pinned my faith upon
the delufions of life :—I believed in the pro-
feffions of the Great, I believed that there
were friends, that there were benefactors,
that there were men of probity, that there
were men of compaffion, that there were men
of fouls -fo expanded as to love. Virtue for
her own fake—I believed that every thing was
what it ought to be, and what it is not. My
father's fortune, already narrow, became
daily more fo. My fifter had married a
gentleman, who though not in opulent,
was yet in eafy, circumftances. As for
myfelf, I had inherited, with my life, an
elevation of foul wholely repugnant to what
is termed the art of pufhing one's fortune.
My delicacy in this point was perhaps too
fcrupulous; but I concluded, that my
friends (for friendfhip was my favourite
chimera), would love me ftill more for the
independency of my difpofition. My com-

pany

pany was univerfally courted; and I made it my ftudy to deferve, not only the efteem which they feemed to lavifh upon me, but, what is of greater confequence, the efteem of myfelf. I fpeak not of the women: of them I have infinitely lefs to complain than of the men. Woman can throw a grace over her moft ftriking imperfections; and we lofe fight of her ficklenefs, her frivolity, in the contemplation of her charms, and that tincture of foftnefs and humanity which beams through all her actions. She prefents not, in all its deformity, like man, a picture of infolence and of cruelty.

There was another delufion which I delighted to indulge. I imagined that a rich man ought not to know, to relifh, another happinefs but that of rendering himfelf ufeful, of diffufing around his benefits. I began to perceive, that I ought to think ferioufly about myfelf——to perceive, that Want approached to me with hafty fteps.

K 2

I was

I was told, that I was a man of talents, and that it would be eafy for me to bid defiance to my cruel deftiny.——What fhall I tell you, Sir?—I had now reached the period in which I was to behold Man as he is. My father informed me, that, by the iffue of a law-fuit, in which he had been engaged, he was ruined.—Alas! a juft claim had been his only fupport.——I waited not for the call of duty:—inclination told me what to do. For fome years I employed every honourable method to foften for my worthy parent the rigours of indigence. He was poor; and I felt him cling to my heart yet more clofely than ever. Admitted into the circles of the great, I flattered myfelf that they would be melted with my forrows. Without blufhing for my fituation, or fwelling with a ridiculous pride, which often, as a prop, is affumed by Adverfity, I difcovered to them my melancholy cafe, and enlarged upon the tears,

the

the venerable wrinkles, of my father. In their promises, they assumed a familiar dignity, and displayed to me all the pride, all the ostentation, of protectors—to me, who thought I should have debased them, if I had descended so low as to appear in the character of a dependent. Madman that I was, I loved them; and it is impossible to love but when our souls feel a certain equality, without which no friendship, no social pleasure whatever, can exist. These slaves of the court had slaves under them, more unnatural an hundred times than their worthless masters; and they made me drink of the cup of sorrow and humiliation even to the dregs. This first trial pierced me with indignation. Would you believe, that one of those *Greatlings* cried aloud one day, to a number of his companions, in answer to some affecting and pathetic complaints which dropped from me, " It would be a " pity, that this fellow should make his for-

" tune—

" tune—he is really amuſing with his com-
" plaints: they give a vivacity to his ima-
" gination which produces the moſt agree-
" able ſallies ?"—

Unwilling to ſerve as a ſpectacle, or to cheriſh the brutal frivolity of theſe poliſhed barbarians, I determined to apply to my friends in the literary world; not doubting but that in them I ſhould find thoſe ſentiments which I had in vain looked for in their pretended Mecenaſes. Theſe preceptors of mankind, thought I, who are perpetually writing encomiums upon Virtue, muſt be completely virtuous.———On the theatre they adorn her with all the charms of wit and genius.—How cordial will be my reception from thoſe philoſophers, thoſe ſages, whoſe whole employment is, to alleviate the evils of humanity—humanity, a word, with which they give a ſanction to every page they write!———I flew to them

with

with a becoming confidence, and bedewed, but in vain, their bosoms with my tears.— With grief I found, that Wit was an impostor, who could assume any mask—found, that those panegyrists of Virtue were a kind of empyrics, who having hung out signs to catch the admiration of the multitude, laugh in their sleeves at the success of their devices——found, that their hearts were hardened by system ; that, when reputation, or interest, was not at stake, they were strangers to those ideas of legislation and virtue, which, with so much pomp, they lay down in their writings ; that, in a word, they were the slaves of envy, of vanity, and of ambition.

Here are already two different characters presented to me in their naked colours. I will not detain you with an enumeration of every circumstance more cruel than another which befel me. I received a thousand

affronts,

affronts; my heart was wounded in a thoufand places. To thefe ftrokes, heavy and
cutting as they are, the unfortunate are an
unceafing prey. As to the rich, my rage
kindles with the bare idea of them. They
are proftituted to every vice, to every crime.
Nothing can equal their infolence but their
inhumanity. They even affect not to conceal that their hearts are of iron; while the
great endeavour to foften the rigour of their
difpofitions by an exterior fhow of polite-
nefs.———It would feem, that, to acquire
wealth, was to acquire a privilege to renounce
the duties of a man; that, in the eyes of
fuch wretched favourites of Fortune, the
moft agreeable, the moft engaging, objects
are, the fufferings and the tears of the unhappy. The fierceft animals are lefs cruel.
If the unfortunate would, at any time, forget the horrors of their fituation, let them
fhun the fociety of the rich, let them rather hope for relief from the meaneft of
indigents.

indigents. From thefe they will at leaft obtain pity, that healing balfam for the wounds of the heart.

No perfon can have the effrontery to fay, that I beheld not in their true light thofe monfters whom opulence has hardened; that becaufe I hate them, I have loaded them with the moft outrageous difdain. A ftupid cit might think, might feel, if he could only throw off that fpirit of imitation, which renders him the ape of his fuperiors, and which infpires him with a paffion for luxury, the bane of fentiment and of virtue. His every thought, his every pleafure, his exiftence itfelf, centers in his money, by the amount of which he calculates the amount of his happinefs, and of his reputation.

As for the people, as they are termed, they are merely animated clay; and a fordid

intereft,

intereft, whofe rude mechanifm we can eafily manage, is their principle of action. They will weep at a ftory of diftrefs; and in the fame inftant they will ftab to the heart the haplefs fubject of it, if, by his death, they may earn a fhilling more than by their labours.

At length I had examined every ftation in life, yet ftill I longed to find a Man.—Oh! thought I, fenfibility is furely to be met with among thofe who, fecluded from the vanities of the world, profefs the religion of a benevolent God, before whom they daily prefent themfelves, in order to root in them the true fpirit of chriftianity.—More humiliations, Sir, were yet in ftore for me.—Here I found an utter fterility of fen-timent, found rigour in the extreme. There is no inhumanity fo barbarous as that which affumes the form of piety. The comforts I received now were more mortifying, more cutting, than the moft bitter affronts.—

How

How abominable is the compaffion of a falfe devotee !—

In the heighth of fury, and of defpair, I threw myfelf at the feet of my parent.

" Oh ! my father," cried I, " we are reduced to the moft dreadful extremity.——I flattered myfelf, that in my youth you would find a prop—but all my hopes are vanifhed.— Every heart is impenetrable to my tears— my tears, which flow for you alone.—Alas ! my dear, my venerable, father, what will become of you?"—

" Whatever heaven fhall decree," returned the worthy old man.—"Would it be a hardfhip for me to die? No :—I have already reached the end of my career.——It is for thee that I now weep: my happinefs, my life, was wrapped up in thee ; and now when I am on the point of perifhing, I have

nothing

nothing to leave to thee but tears and misfortunes.—O my dear son, could I have believed that mankind were thus infenfible!—
Go, and difturb not thyfelf about my fate:
feek only to preferve—what in reality is
mine—your own exiftence; and leave me
upon the brink of my grave, into which I
will fink without a pang, if thus I may ap-
peafe the Almighty, thus I may render my
child happy."—

With thefe words my fobbing father took
me in his arms, and preffed me to his
breaft.——Alas! Sir, the fcene is ftill before me.

It is needlefs to repeat to you every humiliating and ineffectual ftep to which I
demeaned myfelf, every degree of calamity
which I underwent, and which plunged me
yet more deeply into mifery. I thought
of nothing but the diftreffes of my
father :

father : thefe were the only objects of my attention, the only fpring of my actions. When my circumftances were tolerable, I had done fervices to a number of perfons whom I thought my friends; but hardly had I difcovered a fymptom of adverfity, when they all, like vapours, vanifhed from my fight, leaving me a fpectacle of ingratitude and malice feafting upon my deftruction, and the deftruction of my father.

One refource ftill remained to us. My brother-in-law loved my fifter.—She had received from my father the moft tender proofs of affection; and I never once doubted but that fhe would prevail with her hufband to fnatch us from the jaws of poverty. I waited upon her, but told not my father of my intention. She received me with a coldnefs which the warmth of my own heart would not allow me to perceive. As I communicated to her my errand, her

looks

looks became gradually lefs endearing and lefs familiar:—her infenfibility betrayed her, and difplayed itfelf upon her countenance.

She replied to me, that her hufband was engaged in building, and that he had children.—"My father," fhe addded, "has had no conduct:——he has obliged relations and friends, who are now richer than we are— let him difclofe his fituation to them.— And you with your talents, how comes it that you are unprovided for? You will never have the fpirit to raife your fortune."—

" I will never have a heart of iron, the heart of an unnatural fifter," interrupted I.— "Adieu, barbarous woman! —Your father is ready to die of want, and you will not relieve him—you, whom he loves with fo much tendernefs!—Away, wretched creature!—May your children not punifh you for this crime!—Henceforth you fhall never fee

me

me more.—Ungrateful fister, I afked no-thing of you for myfelf—it was"—

Here, choaked with tears, I burft from her hateful prefence. I endeavoured to conceal from my father this new difafter; but my heart was oppreffed with it, and it efcaped from me.

"Ah! my father," cried I, "hear the caufe of my abfence from you thefe few days.—I thought, that you had ftill a daughter, that I had ftill a fifter.—Alas! fhe is a monfter of inhumanity.—She has refufed us the fmalleft fuccour, yet it is to you that fhe owes her life, and every bleffing fhe enjoys!"—

" It is doubtlefs," replied the courageous old man, " a dreadful calamity to be treated with cruelty by thofe who derive their exiftence from us: it is the completion of mifery.—But God, and my fon," continued

he—

he—covering me with his filver locks, and with his tears—" are ftill my comforters:—to them I will breathe forth my laft figh.— We muft forgive thy fifter—fhe is depend- ent upon her hufband, and upon her child- ren."—

" Her children !—Ah ! my father, thefe ought to make her feel your rights."—

Alas! Sir, as yet I have told you no- thing.—My father, my wretched father, is dragged to prifon.—I throw myfelf at the feet of his creditor; and he fpurns me from him with fiercenefs—fpurns me, and I did not deftroy him ! My fenfibility was wholely engroffed by the fituation of my father. The fmalleft affiftance, hu- man or divine, was denied me. My trifling effects I fold. Paint to yourfelf, Sir, the horrid picture of our woes : my father in confinement; miferably perifh-

ing

ing in it, bereft of every support but that of his wretched son, who was himself abandoned by the world, was himself stripped of every thing, and surrounded with monsters and with precipices.——I am a gentleman, Sir—my soul is elevated, is incapable of meanness. What I did was for an aged father, whose last breath I seemed to preserve. I sacrificed myself, I subdued my pride. Nature cried aloud to me; and to relieve my wretched parent, I embraced the most debasing situation.—— Would you believe it, Sir?—

Here the voice of Silli became inarticulate with tears and with sobs.

Would you believe it, Sir?—By the cruelty of my fellow-creatures I was reduced to the necessity of begging alms for the author of my being. Every night, with a voice drowned in tears, with a voice of the

moſt gloomy ſorrow, did I implcre the pity
of monſters, whoſe hearts I could with pleaſure have torn.——

At theſe words Sidney, with tears flow-
ing down his checks, claſped the ſtranger in
his arms.

"O noble creature!" exclaimed he—
"how beautiful is your ſoul!—how deſerv-
ng are you of friends!"—

I counted theſe alms, continued the other--
alms!—what a word, Sir!—I counted them
with ſo many pieces of my heart, which
ſeemed to loofen from within me.——With
this reſource, ignominious and feeble as it
was, I had, however, the comfort to preferve the remnant of my father's life.

Still did the ſcourge of Fortune hang over
me, I was ſeized as a vagrant, who begs not
but

but to encourage his bafe idlenefs and
floth.  It is for my father—it is for my father, that I have defcended to this meannefs, cried I to the tigers who furrounded
me:—he is in prifon, and his life depends
upon my carrying to him fome prefent affiftance.—In the name of humanity, of—

Deaf to my fupplications, they hurried
me along—hurried me, and threw me into a
dungeon.  I infifted on being carried before
a magiftrate.  When I appeared before my
judge, he affumed a ftern countenance, and
put fuch queftions to me as if I had been
upon the point of condemnation.

"Alas! Sir," pronounced I, "that I am a
beggar is true; yet am I not formed to appear in that ignominious character.—Sprung
from a family of diftinction, I might, perhaps, like other perfons in a fimilar fituation, have had the audacity to put a period



to

to my exiſtence, if——Sir, I have a father, a father overwhelmed with miſery, and in priſon.——It is for him, it is for the being who gave birth to me, that I applied for charity."————

The magiſtrate was affected ; and having ſigned my diſcharge, he promiſed me a protection, of which his death prevented me from enjoying the fruits.

Age proved at length a ſuccefsful advocate for my father. The laws unbarred to him the gates of his priſon ; and he again enjoyed the bleſſing of liberty. I obtained an appointment in an Eaſt-India veſſel, by which I might, with difficulty, obtain a ſubſiſtence. In my arms I ſupported my father, till I got him on ſhip-board.

" Come, my dear, my wretched, parent," ſaid I to him ; " let us leave this land of guilt;

let us leave the favages of Europe:—the tigers of Afia will, perhaps, be lefs cruel to
us. While I have wherewithall to fupport
my own deplorable days, you, O my father!
fhall live.——Alas! I have not a friend
but you! You are my only care: let us
forget the very name of our country."—

Still have I related to you but a portion
of my forrows: my heart was acquainted
with others, which, next to thofe I felt for
the fituation of the author of my days, were
the moft bitter of all. In a ftate of diftrefs
the foul is more fufceptible of the impreffions
of tendernefs than in a ftate of happinefs.
Misfortune is attended with a melancholy
which gives birth to the greateft paffions.—
In a word, I dared to love.—I will fupprefs
a minute detail of what I ought to banifh
from my remembrance. The object of my
paffion was a young woman, an only daugh-

ter,

ter, who was entitled to a fortune which raifed her above my hopes. Reafon, honour, commanded me to be filent, and to fubdue a paffion which it was denied me to infpire. I liftened neither to reafon, nor to my fitu-ation—I liftened to love; and Julia, (fo the adorable miftrefs of my heart was called) anticipated, in fome meafure, my wifhes. Regardlefs of confequences, we confeffed to each other our mutual flame. Love dried up my tears, and enabled me to fuftain the load of life. A relation of the lady read in our hearts; for young perfons are unfkilled in the arts of diffimulation. He defired, that we might have a private interview; and thus he addreffed himfelf to me.

" You will not, I hope, Sir, be offended at the freedom with which I fhall exprefs my fentiments to you.—I believe you to deferve the efteem of every worthy perfon :—your birth is refpedable, your

figure

figure is engaging; and I perceive that my niece entertains the fame fentiments of you that I do myfelf.—Your foul feems to be refined, and acquainted with the dictates of honour.--You have no fortune, my niece will have fome, therefore"————

"It is enough, Sir," interrupted I, with warmth.—"I feel my duty, my misfortunes; and you fhall know what I am."—

I hurried away, in order to write a letter to Julia; and it was at the very inftant that my father and I were taking our leave of that part of the world where my love re-fides.—Thefe were the contents of it.

"I love you, adorable Julia, and will
" not ceafe to love you through life. To
" the excefs of my tendernefs for you im-
" pute it that I have ever difclofed to you the
" fentiments of a heart, which ought to be a
" ftranger

" ftranger to every paffion but that of for-
" row for being denied the poffeffion of
" you.—Divine creature, I am encompaffed
" with poverty.—Let me appear without
" vanity in the eyes of Julia.—It is not for
" me, the moft wretched of men, to hope,
" for your hand.  Forget me—forget me,
" thou miftrefs of my foul.—What have I
" faid?—But I muft fay it.—Yes, Julia,
" tear my image from your heart—tear it,
" and be the happinefs of your relations,
" the happinefs of——of the hufband whom
" Fortune fhall throw into your arms.  I
" now bid adieu to Europe—bid adieu to
" Julia.——Enquire not about what fhall
" have become of me in thofe countries to
" which my cruel deftiny may lead me.
" While it is permitted me to live, my foul
" will be full of you.—After Julia what
" woman can triumph there?——Adieu !—
" Adieu !—Once more let me conjure you
" to forget me:—your duty and my honour--
" your own happinefs, requires it."

I wet

I wet this letter with my tears—wet it, and would have added to it a thoufand things. At length I fet fail with my father, who now engaged all my tendernefs, all my attention; and it was during our voyage that I difcovered to him my unhappy paffion. On our arrival in this country, having been deprived of my employment by the artifices of a villain, I again funk into the moft wretched indigence. I prayed for affiftance to all around me with cries, and with tears; I fhewed them the venerable wrinkles of my parent, his grey hairs, his grave ready to open for him. Every eye was turned from me, every heart was fhut.— Alas! there is no humanity on earth. The monfters of India are not lefs cruel than the monfters of Europe. At length we crawled into a cavern on the borders of the fea.— There, while I beheld my wretched father gradually confumed with hunger, I covered him with kiffes, I preffed him to my heart;

and,

and, calling Nature to my aid, I obtained
a momentary relief for him in the juice of
some herbs which I expressed upon his
parched and dying lips.  He had no sooner
breathed his laft, than grief, despair, rage,
took possession of my senfes.  As I rushed
from the cavern in a frenzy, I perceived a
party of Indians who were about to engage
with the Europeans—the Europeans, who
are the particular objects of my hatred, my
indignation, who pretend to know by education the duties of Nature, who pronounce
themselves the most exalted of the human
race.——You were a witness of my fury,
my madness:  I would have destroyed all
nature.——My father is dead—dead of hunger !——Alas! Sir, why did you preserve
my life?——Permit me to rid myself of a
burthen  I can  no  longer  endure.  You
know all my misfortunes:—how can I repair them but in death?—You seem to me
to be different from men, from those barbarians—

barians—you feem to be acquainted with pity. What greater benefit then can you render me than not to prolong my exift- ence?"——

" No, worthy youth," returned Sidney, embracing him—" you fhall not die.—You have found a heart, a friend.—Think not that all men are monfters of inhumanity :— you fhall be convinced that there are fome who are endowed with fenfibility and ten- dernefs.—In me you fhall find a father.— What is your name ?"—

" My name, Sir, is Silli."—

"Well, my dear Silli, you fhall be my fon--

"Ah ! my dear benefactor !—My father, my father—alas ! he is no more."——

Sidney redoubled his tender affiduity, in order to reftore the unhappy youth to a life he hated.

Come,

" Come," faid he to him, two days after his health had begun to return—" I long to reconcile you with mankind.——— Here, my friend, give me your arm."—

And he conducted him to a neighbouring tent.

What a fcene prefented itfelf!

" My father !—Do I then hold you in my arms !" cried Silli.

Scenes of this kind baffle defcription.

The Frenchman had funk upon the bofom of an old man, who could only utter, " O my fon, my dear child !"—

Sometimes he embraced Silli, fometimes he covered with kiffes the hand of Sidney.

Generous

"Generous ftranger!" cried he, "you have reftored to me my fon—have reftored two fouls to each other.—Enjoy the fight—a fight, which is worthy of a God, which is the bleffed fruit of your benevolence."—

Silli opened his eyes.

Still, my father, do I behold thee!—Still art thou alive!—

"He is, my dear Silli; and it is I who am fo happy as to give you this proof of friendfhip.—I flew myfelf to the cavern you mentioned; and there I found your venerable father in the arms of a Banyan, who had brought fome nourifhment to him, and who was exerting his efforts to recall him into life.—You fee that even in India there are Men.———I gave orders that he fhould be brought hither:—live both of you, and love me."—

Love!

"Love! we will adore you as our supreme benefactor, interrupted the old man.—Yes, my son," said he, turning to Silli—" to this gentleman I owe my life, and the pleasure of embracing thee. When at the point of expiring, I raised my eye-lids to look for thee, and I beheld a stranger. He put into my mouth a liquor, which revived my spirits, and food, which gave me strength; but still I saw not my dear son.——Here then is the second support of my old age," added he, as he attempted to prostrate himself at the feet of Sidney.

" What are you about, my father?" cried our generous countryman.—"I am infinitely more happy than you. I have obliged two worthy hearts.—Henceforth consider me as your faithful friend.——The English"—

And he gave a smile of benevolence.

" The English are not always at war with the French."—

Silli

Silli and his father had not words to exprefs their gratitude. When they faw Sidney, when they fpoke to him, they fhed
thofe tears, thofe fweet tears, which are the
tribute of the heart.—O happy Sidney!
and how deferving waft thou of thy happinefs !——

" I have yet done nothing, my friends,"
faid he to them, one day:—" it is not enough
that I have preferved your lives, if I put you
not in a fituation to enjoy them. Thus fituated, exiftence would be a burthen to you :
my work is only begun, and I long to complete it.——Did you not tell me, worthy
youth," continued he, addreffing himfelf to
Silli, " that you had contracted a paffion for
a young woman who amply merited your
love ?"—

" Ah ! my dear benefactor, love muft die
in my bofom.—I will not give place to another

other fentiment, another fenfation, but that of gratitude.—Gratitude fhall engrofs my heart; and poor will be its recompence for all I owe to you.

"My dear child—for I entertain for you the fentiments of a father—my dear child," refumed Sidney, "it is my intention, I repeat it, to render you happy.—And could you be happy while you poffeffed not the woman of your heart?——Believe me, I am no ftranger either to the pleafures or the pains of love.—On my return to Europe, I fhall go to Paris; and you fhall accompany me thither."—

They foon quitted India. From the attention, the favours, which Sidney beftowed upon the two Frenchmen, one would have thought, that the old man was his father, that Silli was his brother. Often did our hero of benevolence furprife the latter gazing upon the fea in melancholy, and

fhedding

shedding tears. The image of Julia had
assumed a more unbounded empire in his
soul than ever; and as he advanced towards
Europe, the corroding anguish of his heart
encreased.

" Whither am I going?" said he to himself
one day, absorbed in silent grief.--" To behold
the happiness of another in the possession of
the charms of Julia—to behold her love for
him ?——Ought I not rather to fly from
France for ever?—Ought I not to follow
my dear benefactor to England ?—Have I
another country but his ?—Shall I not háve
the resolution to fly from a land which I
ought to detest ?—I want to see Julia !—
And for what reason, unhappy wretch ?—
Haft thou not yet sufficiently exhausted thy
evil fortune ? What madness hurries thee
to meet the fatal blow that waits for thee ?--
And if Julia was not married, could I hope
to become her husband ?——Belongs it to
me to abuse the goodness of Sidney ?—

M

Would!

Would it not be the heighth of ingratitude to put his benevolence to new trials?"—

The laſt words he pronounced aloud.

"No, ſaid Sidney"—whom he had not obſerved—"no," ſaid he, as he embraced him, "you muſt not be afraid of wearing out the friendſhip of a man whom you have obliged in preſenting him with an opportunity of exerting his ſenſibility."—

"You are a being from heaven!" exclaimed Silli with warmth.

"I am your friend, reſumed Sidney."—

At length they reached Paris; and Silli, impelled by love, flew to the abode of Julia. There he was informed, that her father was dead, that her circumſtances had undergone a melancholy change, and that the young lady and her mother lived together in an

obſcure

obſcure retreat, unknown to the world. After much enquiry, he traced them out.—— What objects preſented themſelves to his view!——Julia, his dear Julia, ſurrounded with the moſt humiliating diſtreſs, and at work, in order to ſupport her own wretched exiſtence, and that of her mother.

" Ah! my dear Julia!" cried Silli, throwing himſelf at her feet.

At the ſight of her lover, Julia gave a ſhriek, and ſunk in a ſwoon upon the boſom of her mother, who was herſelf motionleſs with aſtoniſhment and with joy.

" Is it you, Sir!" ſaid ſhe.—"You behold in a ſituation widely different from that in which you left us."——

" I behold you," interrupted Silli, "more worthy than ever of my reſpect, my homage.——What! my dear Julia, is ſhe too the victim of Fortune!"——



In

In the mean while fhe had recovered her fenfes.—We have no language to exprefs the tranfports of two hearts, which are impreffed with the moft warm, the moft affectionate, love for each other, and whofe union is confirmed by misfortune. The two unhappy ladies related to Silli all their afflictions. Neglected by their relations, and expofed to the moft abject poverty, every bofom was fhut againft their tears. Sometimes they talked of Silli; and the repetition of his name alleviated their forrows.—"Alas!" would Julia fay, " if he is yet alive, his heart is full of us—he thinks, that I am happy."—

"Ah! Silli," exclaimed fhe, in concluding her narrative—"your prefence throws an oblivion over our misfortunes.—You fee our cruel fituation:—I am obliged to work, in order to preferve the life of my venerable mother, and my own life, on which her's depends."—

See!

"See!" refumed Silli—"I fee, that diftrefs has rendered Julia an hundred times more beautiful, more refpectable, more worthy of adoration, than ever.——Ah! my dear friends—indulge me in this expreffion of the foul—there are beings, then, on whom heaven exhaufts its wrath!—Inconceivable fatality!—My heart is your's—yes, I will dry up your tears—will drag you from this abyfs of mifery."—

And he haftened to his father. Sidney was with him.

"O, my father—my exalted friend! I have found Julia—found her in mifery, but more beautiful, more amiable, than ever."—

He defcribed their fituation; and with his own tears he feemed to convey thofe of Julia and her mother.

Come,

" Come, my friend ! " interrupted Sidney haftily—" away with the gloomy picture !—Is it not your wifh to marry Julia ?"—

" Marry her, Sir !—to the empire of the world would I promote her, if Fortune would make it mine.—But how fhall our deftinies be united ?—O heaven ! misfortune is the only tie that can ever unite us.—If I might but relieve them from this humiliating indigence !"—

" And do you doubt that you might ?" replied our worthy countryman, in an affecting, a heart-fprung, accent.—Forget you, that Sidney is your friend ?"—

" My noble benefactor, if you beheld her, if you beheld Julia and her mother, you would become acquainted with mifery in all its dignity, in all its extent."—

Sidney

Sidney ftaid to fup with Silli and his fa_
ther.—Twenty times did he embrace them,
did he, with his eyes, exprefs to them a certain tendernefs which is the foul of friendfhip.

" Remember," faid he.———

And he clafped the hands of both.

"Remember, that I am the party obliged.--
I have had it in my power to be ferviceable
to two of my fellow creatures : to you it is
owing that I have; and I efteem it the fum-
mit of happinefs.———Forget not to love
me.———Let Sidney abide always in your
hearts :—his heart will be always open to
you.———In England," added he, turning to
the old man, "you fhall have an affectionate,
a refpectful, fon; and you, my dear Silli, a
warm brother and friend.—

Before he took his leave, he clafped them
repeatedly in his arms—clafped them, and
with

with tears pronounced, " For what pleafure am I indebted to you !"—

· The next morning, as the two French-men were preparing to wait upon their be-nefactor, Silli received a letter from Sidney. It was couched in thefe terms :

" My affairs recall me into England;
" and I leave you, my worthy friends, fome
" proofs of a friendfhip which I fhall carry
" with me to the grave. Young Silli, to
" you I addrefs myfelf. In the fchool of
" adverfity you have acquired wifdom.
" With greater eafe, therefore, will you
" liften to reafon, will you know the value
" of that mediocrity which is the feat of
" real happinefs and of virtue. Marry Julia;
" enjoy with your father the fweets of
" friendfhip; and with him complete a
" family of worthy people which may ferve
" as an example to mankind. I would
" have begged of you to introduce me to
                                        " Julia,

" Julia, if I had not been apprehenſive, that
" my preſence would have been leſs agree-
" able to her, and to her mother, than
" theirs would have been intereſting to me.
" They are in diſtreſs; and diſtreſs requires
" a certain reſpect which I need not de-
" ſcribe to you who know it ſo well.—
" Adieu, my friends.—You ſhall hear from
" me; and on whatever land my fate ſhall
" throw me, I ſhall continue to love you.
" Tell me not of gratitude; it is I who
" ſhall feel it, if you will ſo far eſteem me
" as to conſider my feeble ſervices as your
" due.

" P. S. To-morrow morning you will
" receive the ſum of five thouſand pounds."

Silli had hardly read the laſt word, when
a ſtranger waited upon him with caſh and
notes to the above amount.

The old man and he remained ſpeechleſs
with joy, with aſtoniſhment, and with gratitude.

O heavenly

" O heavenly heart !" exclaimed the fon at length.—" And do'ft thou fly from our adorations, from our tears !—How thou embittereft to us thy benefits in depriving us of the comfort of throwing ourfelves at thy feet, of idolizing thee as the model of benevolence !——Go, our hearts fhall accompany thee wherever thou art."—

" Angelic foul !" cried the old man.—My dear fon, what a being !—Ah! he belongs not to the race of man !——Sidney, we would expire with gratitude at thy feet !—

Indeed, if there exifts not fuch benevolence as that of the generous Sidney, there exift not fuch feeling, fuch grateful, hearts as thofe of the two Frenchmen. Conceive the eagernefs with which young Silli flew to his miftrefs. He was happy, becaufe he had it in his power to efpoufe his Julia, to confer happinefs on every thing

that

that was dear to him. He purchafed a little eftate in the country; and thither he retired with his wife, with his father, and with the mother of Julia. Every day, every moment, heightened his felicity, heightened his thankfulnefs. He bleffed the Supreme Being and Sidney in every thing he poffeffed : in every thing did he trace the image of his benefactor, did he feel the infpiration of gratitude. Silli now acknowledged, that misfortune hath its period, that virtue hath, even on earth, its reward; that there are men who are an honour to humanity. In confideration of the benevolent Englifhman, he forgave every cruelty he had fuftained. His foul foftened; he became a true philofopher; and every object prefented itfelf to him in its proper colour.

They frequently received letters from Sidney; and in their anfwers to him they breathed out their fouls in the moft pure, the

moft

moſt lively, ſentiments.  Sidney made a
ſecond voyage to India; a circumſtance,
which, as it interrupted their correſpon-
dence, oppreſſed their feeling and generous
hearts with perpetual alarms for the ſafety
of their friend.——Every Engliſhman was
dear to them.——At length they received
intelligence that Sidney was no more.  This
was a thunder-bolt to the whole family.  The
old man, as if unable to ſurvive the fatal
tidings, fell ſick, and was reduced to the
laſt extremity.  The ſon, ſurrounded with
his wife, and his children, no longer felt a
pleaſure in their careſſes, no longer entertained a wiſh but for death.  In his deſpair
the name of Sidney was his only language.
Julia reminded him of his family, who had
not a ſupport but in him, and he, in ſome
meaſure, recovered—recovered, to drag on a
life of wretchedneſs, to ſhun the ſociety
of man in the retreats of ſolitude and
of gloom.

Ah!

" Ah ! Sidney," exclaimed he, one day, in the heart of a little wood, adjoining to the highway, where he was feated at the foot of a tree, with his head drooping towards the ground, and oppreffed with a death-like melancholy—" Ah ! Sidney, fhall I then never fee thee more !—Shall I never more prefs thee to my heart—my heart, which is more than ever impreffed with thy favours !——Angelic foul, do'ft thou hear me ?—Do'ft thou behold my tears, the tears of my family ?  O ! my dear Sidney"——

" He is in thy arms," cried a man, as he flew to embrace him.

It was Sidney himfelf.

" Sidney !" pronounced the other.

And that inftant he fainted away.

" Yes, my dear Silli, it is Sidney, thy friend, who has returned from the extremity

of

of the earth to embrace thee, and to offer thee new fervices," refumed Sidney, while two rivulets of tears flowed down his cheeks.—" Informed by a peafant that thou waft in this wood, I difmiffed my equipage that I might have the pleafure of thus furprifing thee."—

" Is it you, is it my dear Sidney, whom I thus embrace!" cried Silli as he recovered his fenfes.—" Ah! you muft fee the fruits of your benevolence—muft fee my child-ren—Mine! they are your's alfo."—

And he called to one of his fervants, who remained at a little diftance, upon the road.

" Run inftantly to my houfe, and tell my father, my wife, my children—tell them, that here my benefactor is, that here they muft come, and throw themfelves at his feet.—My friend! and do I embrace thee!— What joy!——But why did I receive the killing news of thy death?"——

" I fhall

" I fhall inform you," replied Sidney :—
" in the mean while, let us haften to your
" dear family."——

Having arrived almoft as foon as the do-
meftic, they entered the apartment of old
Silli, whofe ftrength would hardly permit
him to ftretch out his arms to Sidney, and
to exclaim, " O, my dear fon ! my worthy
friend !"—

Silli, the charming Julia, who was not
yet twenty-five years old, and three children, the oldeft of whom was about fix,
knelt with one accord at the feet of Sidney,
embraced his knees, and repeated, "Our dear
benefactor !" while Sidney, raifing them up,
preffed them to his heart, and wept over
them.

This is the fpectacle which Virtue enjoys
—this is her reward.

" My

"My dear wife, my dear children,"
cried Silli, " you now behold your real
husband, your real father, the author of
your days, and of the happineſs you enjoy.—Do homage to him: adore the Almighty Being by adoring a ſoul that is an
image of himſelf.———O, my dear Sidney!
enjoy the ſweets of benevolence in their utmoſt extent."—

Sidney extolled the beauty, the artleſs
graces, of Julia: ſhe was Virtue herſelf
with the features of Love. He took the
little innocents in his arms, who ſmiled
upon him with a charm peculiar to their
infant years.

"Well did my dear papa" cried the
eldeſt one—and he beſtowed upon Sidney
his little endearing careſſes as he ſpoke to
him—"well did my dear papa recommend
it to us, that we ſhould pray to God for you
every

every day of our lives.—You, he tells us, are our father likewife."—

How endearing was this homage!—What rapture did it excite in the breaft of the magnanimous Sidney!—To evince their gratitude to him, was the fole bufinefs of Silli, and of his family.

He continued feveral weeks with his friends, during which period the old man recovered his health, and with it, in fome meafure, the vigour of youth. They related to each other every circumftance that had befallen them; in the courfe of which it appeared, that Sidney had been attacked with an illnefs fo alarming, that the report of his death was univerfal. To this accident it was owing, that the above unhappy news had reached the ears of his friends in Europe. Silli, on his part, entered into the moft minute particulars with

his benefactor. Prompted by the example
of the Englifh, he had engaged in commerce, in order to obtain for himfelf, and
for his family, an honourable independence.
Though a gentleman, and a Frenchman, he
yet blufhed not to affume a character,
which in itfelf is infinitely preferable to
that of a neglected lounger in the ante-
chambers of grandeur, and of opulence. Every
day he ftaid did the happinefs of Sidney
encreafe. Silli opened to him his foul, and
difplayed to him the ferenity, the content,
of it.—He was no longer a fierce mifan-
thrope, an enemy of mankind ; he was an
enlightened philofopher, who, from the
bottom of his heart, ceafed not to utter
thanks to God, and to Sidney, his benefactor. Another happinefs he had enjoyed.
His fifter had been reduced to a dependence
upon his bounty ; and, by affifting her, he
had obtained the moft delicious revenge.
The noble fimplicity of his foul fhone

throughout

throughout his family. His duties and his pleafures engaged the whole of his time. Of thefe his chief were, to love his wife, to educate his children, to inftill into them all his own virtues, all the virtues of his fpoufe, and their mutual tendernefs for Sidney.

On the day which was to precede the departure of their generous patron, they prepared a fumptuous entertainment, toward the clofe of which a large pie was brought upon the table. Silli having preffed his friend to open it, he complied, and found—how great was his aftonifhment!—found a heap of louis d'ors.

" My dear Sidney !" cried Silli, throwing himfelf round the neck of his benefactor—" here are the five thoufand pounds which you lent me with fo much generofity.—By their encreafe I have attained a
fituation

ſituation equal to my wiſhes: this little eſtate is my own, and I have a ſufficiency to bring up a family, who, with their laſt breaths, will bleſs you.—"

" Excellent creatures!" cried Sidney— " Well do you deſerve your good fortune.— And am I ſo happy as to have contributed to it!—Ah! my dear friends, already have I received my reward.——Theſe five thou- ſand pounds I have employed with ſo much advantage, that I muſt not omit to pay the intereſt of them."—

With theſe words, he divided the ſum into three parts, and preſented one to each of the children.

" My little friends," ſaid he, " reſume your property.—This is the only inſtance in which you muſt diſobey your papa.—Come, do not refuſe it—if you do, you will offend me.——Take it, and embrace me."—

Impreſſed

Impreſſed with the moſt lively gratitude, Silli, his father, his wife, would have compelled their generous patron to receive the money; when he, not ſatisfied with perſiſting in his refuſal, took off a ring, and put it upon the finger of Julia. It was a diamond, and worth two thouſand guineas.

" Madam," ſaid he, " my friend will not be offended that you ſhould wear this feeble pledge of my friendſhip."—

One day, as he traverſed the houſe, according to cuſtom, he happened to puſh open a door adjoining to the cloſet of Silli. With aſtoniſhment he ſaw his own portrait, crowned with flowers, and inſcribed, *Our Benefactor*—— ſaw it, and ſunk back into the arms of his friend.—

" What have I beheld !" exclaimed he.

" An

" An object, which, which, next to God, is entitled to my moſt fervent homage.—Every
day do my father, and the reſt of my family,
come hither to preſent their moſt pure re-
ſpects, to pronounce from their hearts,
' Behold the author of our real being, of
every happineſs we enjoy!'—My dear Sidney, it is the temple of gratitude, and my
children every morning embelliſh it with
flowers. The Chineſe adore the memory
of Confucius, and why ſhould not we adore
the image of the moſt virtuous, the moſt
benevolent, of men?—During your firſt
voyage to France, I had the precaution to
take poſſeſſion of your picture in miniature,
as I found it, one day, among your papers; and it was from that picture that
this was painted. In it I perpetually behold my friend, my adorable Sidney.—"


" Yes," continued his wife, and his
father, as they entered that inſtant, " it is
the

the object of a worship, of which you, generous man, are the object."—

Sidney embraced them, and shed a torrent of tears—tears of a pure, a heavenly,
joy.

" Ah!" cried he to them, " ye angels upon
earth, how superior are your souls to mine!—
My sensibility is not equal to your's.——
Henceforth, my friends, let us not separa-
rate.—I have no wife, no children:—-be
you then my family, my children, the
children of my heart.—I shall only leave
you while I make one other voyage to
India : this done, I will again haften to
your arms."—

Sidney kept his word. They now refide
together in a delightful country, where
he ceafes not to utter the praifes of his
*dear family*. Thus he calls them; and

their

their sentiments of gratitude, and of tendernefs, encreafe every day.

With one voice the company pronounced
Sidney the hero of benevolence. "But,"
added one of us, "Newton, Sir, is ftill
a great man."—

F I N I S.